I hadn't done much kissing at that point. I'd watched plenty of other people, notably my sister and her inane boyfriend, Bart. When I was, like, twelve and starting to go to parties, I practiced on my drinking glass, until my sister blabbed out, right at the breakfast table, "Sarah's kissing her juice!" I told them my lip itched, but not even she believed me. The first person who kissed me was at one of those parties. It was Jeffrey Gerber, a.k.a. the Gerber Baby, a.k.a. Jeffrey the Gerbil, and I didn't kiss him back. I did kiss this other person, Jason, back, but he was such a space cadet, I don't think he knew the difference.

David knew the difference. He leaned very close to me. When his mouth was so close to mine I stopped breathing, he said, very softly, "So we're both nervous."

Lucy Frank lives with her husband and son in New York City. Her first novel was *I Am an Artichoke*.

Will You Be
My Brussels Sprout?

BY LUCY FRANK

Published by
Bantam Doubleday Dell Books for Young Readers
a division of
Bantam Doubleday Dell Publishing Group, Inc.
1540 Broadway
New York, New York 10036

Visit us on the Web! www.bdd.com

Educators and librarians, visit the BDD Teacher's Resource Center at www.bdd.com/teachers

ISBN: 0-440-22734-8

RL: 5.2

Reprinted by arrangement with Holiday House, Inc.

Printed in the United States of America

June 1998

10 9 8 7 6 5 4 3 2 1

OPM

For Peter and Michael

Will You Be
My Brussels Sprout?

Chapter 1

I didn't come to New York City to fall in love. I came for cello lessons. If anyone had told me I'd fall in love with Emily's brother, I'd have said they were insane. One, Emily was almost like a sister to me—a sister with a lot of problems. Two, he was Florence Friedman's son, which opened another whole can of worms.

I'd known Florence and Emily since the summer, when Florence hired me to live with them in New York City as her thirteen-year-old daughter Emily's companion. But David was away working as a camp counselor, so I never met him till six months later on the January morning of my audition. I had decided to stop at the Friedmans' apartment on my way to the conservatory.

"Sarah! Darling!" Before I could put down my cello case, Florence squashed me in a suffocating hug. Florence is large. Buffalo is the image that springs to mind. When Florence hugs you, you know you've been hugged.

And it's not just her body that's outsized; it's her voice, her gestures, her emotions. Even her eyes look huge behind her glasses. "Look at you with your cello! I'm *so* impressed! I wish Emily played an instrument."

"Where is Emily?" I asked, following her to the living room. I'd taken an early train to see Emily, since the music school was only six blocks from her apartment. I'd hardly seen her since Thanksgiving, because she had extra therapy appointments on Saturdays. We talked on the phone, but you couldn't just come out and say, "So, Emily, are you eating?" Even if you could—and especially if you did—she might not tell you. She'd had a problem with anorexia, but that's another story.

"Emily's in the shower." Florence gave me a toothy, overly cheerful smile. "But I want to hear about this new talent of yours. You hid it from me all last summer."

"I didn't hide it," I said. "Last summer I wasn't that interested." I'd taken lessons at school for years, never really getting better, not much caring. But that fall, for some reason, I'd found myself seeking out cello records and practicing without anyone reminding me. And when a cellist came to play at a school assembly, I thought it was the best thing I'd ever heard. I liked it so much I went up afterward and started talking to her. She was the one who gave me this idea of coming to New York for lessons. She said I should see if they'd accept me where she'd studied—the New York Conservatory of Music. It was a college, she explained, but they took younger kids in their prep division.

"I guess my parents figured music was better than most things I could have gotten into," I told Florence. "I figured anything that got me back to the city was a great idea."

"So, do you think they'll take you?" she asked.

"I don't know," I said. "I have no idea how good you have to be."

"Are you any good?"

I shrugged. "I'm one of the best players in the orchestra. Definitely the best cellist. Whatever that means." I put my cello on the couch, unwound my scarf, took off my backpack and my jacket, and dropped them on a chair.

"Not in here!" Florence cried. "Please. Anywhere but here!" The living room was already strewn with books and magazines and papers, but I should have remembered. Florence can handle messes, but only if they're hers. The Friedmans have a huge nine-room apartment and, except for Emily's room, it's always a disaster. "Sweetheart, I'm dying to hear all about your life, but I've got this idiotic astrology article to write." She walked to her computer, pulled a sheet of paper from the printer, looked at it, then crunched it up and threw it on the floor. "Emily will be out any minute. Go on back and make yourself at home."

So I grabbed my things, hoisted the cello strap back onto my shoulder, headed for my old room, and pulled open the door.

"Oops!" I said. I'd forgotten it was David's room. I'd

almost forgotten there was a David. I'd lived in his room the entire summer and barely thought about it. I had been so worried about Emily. Plus I had had this thing for the Friedmans' elevator man, Angel, until he'd joined the Navy in September. Emily still thinks he joined the Navy because of me, but that's also another story.

David was lying on the bed holding a guitar—not playing it, just lying there and staring into space in his pajama top and jeans with shredded knees and those knitted slipper socks with leather soles that grandmas give for Christmas. He was not beautiful like Emily, though his eyes were as big and dark as hers. Unlike the popular guys at school, who are all standard-handsome, groomed and preppy, and tend not to be interested in me, he was too scruffy to be called cute. But there was something about him. Maybe it was the slippers, or his long, reddish, curly hair and glasses. He looked appealing. Also intelligent. Also—corny as this sounds—sensitive.

If I were sensitive, I would have closed the door and left, but for some reason I just stood there. "So, I guess you're David," I said finally. "I'm obviously Sarah."

"Duh," he said.

To further convince him of my intelligence, I added, "Oh, right. You play the guitar."

I was spared another *duh*, because at that point the bathroom door opened, so I called to Emily and made a quick escape.

"I like your sweater," she said, once we were safely in her room and sitting on her bed. She had a towel around her head, so I could see her face was still quite thin, but her arms no longer looked like twigs and she'd lost some of the strained look around her mouth. I was really glad to see her.

"Believe it or not, it's Shelley's," I said. "She's still trying to improve my image." My sister, Shelley, cheerleader and people-person extraordinaire, thinks playing the cello is bad for a sixteen-year-old girl's image, but, as usual, she's wrong. "Your brother thinks I'm a jerk," I said.

"He thinks everyone's a jerk these days," she said, rolling her eyes. "His heart is broken."

"How can you tell?" I said. "To me, he just seemed rude."

"I know." She unwrapped the towel and began combing out her long dark hair. "He hasn't said anything. I mean, he never even came out and told us he had a girlfriend, but I've known about her all along. I even know from the soupy songs he writes that her name's Michelle. And now she's dumped him. The evidence is clear."

"Just because he's lying on his bed wallowing in self-pity?"

She giggled. "That, but also . . ." Her eyes got a mischievous glint, which was a new thing for Emily. Wary used to be her usual expression. "Okay. Let me start from the beginning. Number one: he comes home from that music camp and he's all happy and moony-seeming and he's constantly on the phone and getting all these letters that he won't let anyone see, but which I know he keeps locked up in his desk."

"You read his letters?"

"No, I don't read his letters!" This was a sore point, since Florence was known to read Emily's personal stuff. "But I know that's what he does, because when he couldn't find the key last week, he went ballistic. Number two: he's writing love songs. I hear him through the wall, real late at night, playing his guitar and singing all this stuff about 'your soft lips,' which I know he made up himself, because it never, like, even rhymes. Number three: the whole winter vacation, he's obsessed with whether the mail's come yet and are we absolutely sure there wasn't anything for him. . . ."

I was still thinking about the soft lips, thinking how I'd never been in love, even if Angel had once put his arms around me and kissed my hair, but I said, "Emily, I'm astounded! This is so cool. You're as nosy as I am." She nodded, smiling an I'm-good smile, which was also something new. "He's seventeen, right?"

"Uh-huh. And now, here's the latest part. A few days ago he took my gruesome deaths book, which he denies, but I saw it in his room. So we know he must be feeling really bad."

The book she was referring to was this collection of morbid descriptions of famous people's dying hours. "You're still reading that?" Last summer she practically had it memorized.

She shrugged. "It cheers me up."

"You think he's setting it to music?"

"Shhh!" She put her finger to her lips. "Listen! Do you hear it?" I moved closer to the wall. "He's playing again."

Sure enough, I could hear him strumming his guitar. I couldn't hear any words, just minor chords at first, and then a song, a slow and mournful song, dismal, lugubrious, and strangely familiar-sounding.

"Is he serious?" I said to Emily.

"Why?" she asked.

"That is not a love song. You don't recognize that? Your brother is playing the funeral march version of 'Rudolph, the Red-Nosed Reindeer.'"

"Why are you smiling like that?"

"Like what?" I said.

She gave me a funny look. "Like you're interested."

"In him?" I said. "You're crazy."

Chapter 2

We were so busy talking, I almost forgot about the audition until we got to the conservatory.

It was a good thing I'd talked Emily into walking over with me. The place was a lot scarier than I'd expected. The large, noisy lobby swarmed with kids and every one of them was good. You could tell just by how they walked, the way they held their cases. The orchestra I heard rehearsing was nine million times better than my high-school orchestra. Taped to every wall were homemade flyers announcing student concerts, recitals, and competitions. Next to us, two violinists younger than me discussed what sounded like real jobs with real orchestras. Even the kids so small that their mothers carried their mini-violins looked like prodigies.

My chest felt as if I'd swallowed a volleyball. "Can I leave now?" I asked Emily.

"It's okay, Sarah. You'll be fine." She gave my arm a

pat. "Just remember, okay? *Woof!*" There are several approaches to feeling shaky. One is bad-dog-mode, where you always, automatically, assume you're wrong. Which is what Emily was referring to when she woofed at me. Last summer, we'd made this pact where if one of us heard the other put herself down, she'd bark under her breath. There's also the joke-yourself-out-of-it approach, which, at the moment, had stopped working. A third method, which no doubt comes naturally to some people, is never-let-it-get-to-you.

You can't let this get to you, I told myself as I gave Emily a last pathetic wave and squeezed into the elevator behind a third-grader whose mother was carrying his half-sized cello. You don't know this kid's better than you. You don't know anyone else is better. You've practiced. You learned a new piece this week. You'll be fine.

Right.

For a start, I'd pictured the new teacher as someone young and laid back, like that cellist I'd met at school. Jean Hauptman was not young. She had white hair and no makeup, and she wore a black suit with a silver peacock pin on the collar, silver earrings, and black stockings.

She also was not laid back. "What have you been working on?" she asked. The room was small and square with a baby grand piano, a blackboard with white music staves printed on it, some black metal music stands, and a whole bunch of folding chairs. Her cello was on its side next to the wall.

I said I'd taught myself the "Fauré Elegie" because the pieces Mr. Potter assigned were so uninteresting. "He's not a cellist," I explained. "He just teaches cello. His main instrument is the trombone."

Her frown started when I said that, but the instant I began to play, her forehead really wrinkled. She sat up in her chair. Her eyes bored into me. She leaned toward me as if her whole body was listening for mistakes. I'd barely played two lines when she was up, walking around me, inspecting.

Before I'd even finished the first page of the Fauré, she stopped me. "Let's try a scale," she said. "C major, please; four to a bow, three octaves, very slowly." It's not that she was mean or sneering. More like brisk. Very brisk. "First of all," she said, stopping me after the first octave, "your feet need to be placed squarely in front of you, not wound around the chair legs." She put her hands on my shoulders. "Release your shoulders." She pried at my left thumb. "Let's see if you can relax that death grip on the fingerboard." She pressed down on my right arm. "And let your elbow drop. No, no. Not your left elbow. Your right. Here, let me show you something. Keep playing." She pulled her chair closer to me, sat down again, and grabbed the tip of my bow. "Straight bow. Long and even. No. Let me do the work. Relax."

Just try to relax with someone holding on to your bow and steering it across the string.

A few notes later: "No, no. No vibrato. Never vibrate on scales."

"That's not vibrato," I said. "That's terror." Which it was. I partly said it so she'd laugh or smile or give some sign she liked me, but I was truly shaking.

It took half an hour to get through that scale. Occasionally she'd say, "Good, that's good. You're getting the idea." But then she'd immediately find something else to fix.

Less than twenty-four hours before, I was scooting up and down the fingerboard, sight-reading all kinds of stuff, playing pieces Mr. Potter never taught me. And my sound was good, too. Everyone thought so. Now I could barely play three notes. The C string whuffled like it had been smoking too many cigars, the G string was all gargley, and my high notes were shrill and out of tune. "Excuse me? What was that?" she demanded, each time I was out of tune.

"I sounded much better at home," I said.

"I'm sure you did," she said. She leaned over and picked up a large canvas tote, then stood. A dull gray heaviness settled over me. "I know this is not what you want to hear, Sarah, but you have years of poor teaching, sloppy technique, bad habits, and misconceptions to undo."

I checked my watch. Twenty minutes left and she was packing up to leave. "You're saying I should just go back to Mr. Potter and have him teach me the trombone," I said. I could already hear myself telling my parents I bombed out. Not that they cared. It was easier for them if I took lessons at school. I was the only one who cared.

But she wasn't going to the door. She walked over to her cello, brought it over, and sat down. "Have you ever played these Lee duets?" she said, putting some music on the stand. I shook my head. She leaned forward and opened the book. "They're easy but they're very nice and there's lots to learn in them. Let's hear your A." I played my A string for her and she tuned.

"I've never played any duets," I said. I don't know which I was feeling most right then, beaten up or pissed or relieved that she wasn't walking out on me.

"Oh?" Her eyebrows went up. "Then you're overdue. You'll like these. You take the bottom line." She pulled her chair closer so we could both read off the part.

For the first piece, I was so busy counting I didn't hear a thing. I knew if I screwed up the rhythm she'd jump all over me. But gradually I relaxed enough to listen. I started to hear how the two lines fit together. I started to hear her. I'd thought that cellist who came to school was pretty good, but this was beyond anything I'd ever heard. It was like a person singing, but with a voice so warm and rich and powerful it made my insides hum.

"Now we'll switch," she said when we were done. "You take the top part this time."

I could have listened to her forever, but soon the door opened and a girl walked in with her cello. "Just give us a minute, Natalie," Miss Hauptman said. "Sarah and I have to talk."

"You're so good and I'm so bad," I said, afraid to look at her, dreading what she was going to say.

But as I loosened my bow and pushed my end pin in, she said, "I want you to go to Patelson's and buy yourself some cello methods." She reeled off a list of funny names. "Here, I'll write them down. You need to get to know Patelson's. It's right behind Carnegie Hall. Just get off the train at Fifty-ninth Street on your way downtown. Look over the first ones in the book." She picked up her cello and began to play. "This is the first Popper étude." As she played, she told me what to look for, how to practice. Not one word of it sank in.

"You mean you're actually taking me?" I said. "I should come back next week?"

"I'd say so," she said. And as I zipped my case and hoisted the cello to my shoulder, she added, smiling for what felt like the first time, "It would be a shame to waste those hands on the trombone. Those look to me like cellist's hands."

Chapter 3

"I liked going over to the conservatory with you," Emily told me the next Saturday. I had come in early before my lesson. We had the apartment to ourselves—Florence was out shopping and there was no sign of David. "I liked that I could do something for *you*, for a change."

"You do a lot for me," I said. "You just made me a great brunch." She'd given me two immense blueberry pancakes and hot chocolate with whipped cream, but I'd been too busy telling her about the audition to eat much. I'd told her some of it on the phone, but I wanted her to hear every detail.

"That's not what I mean," she said. She'd served herself one teensy little pancake, tea, and half a grapefruit. She wasn't exactly devouring hers, either. "I mean, like, help you."

"Want to feel my callouses?"

"No thanks."

"C'mon. You said you want to help. Just tell me if you feel anything." I rubbed my thumb against the middle fingertip of my left hand, checking for the hundredth time if the skin was hardening. "They're not like bunions. You want callouses. Real cellists have these, like, knobs, practically, on the ends of their fingers. Miss Hauptman told me." I held my hand out. "There's got to be something forming there. I practiced for an hour and a half every day."

She lightly touched each of my fingertips. "Nothing," she said. "Sorry."

"Well, I'm growing one on my shoulder, if that means anything. From lugging around the stupid cello." That was the bad part: hefting it onto buses, finding seats for it on the train. The good part, I'd discovered, was the way people in New York looked at me, as if I were someone special. "Do you realize that in five years of lessons, Mr. Potter taught me not one right thing?"

"Yes, Sarah," she said. "You've said that several times." I noticed suddenly that she seemed really anxious. "You think you can help me with the math now? I've got that quiz, remember?"

"Oh, right. Sorry." She'd told me that on the phone. That was the main reason she'd invited me.

"It's on inequalities and I don't get it. I can't remember when you switch the inequality; I can't remember greater than and less than, which one points in which direction;

I keep going and going and then it comes back to the same thing. I failed the last one. My dad is going to kill me if I fail again."

"Wait a minute!" I said. "I just read something about math tests. I know you're sick of hearing about music, but there was this thing in the paper about how music can improve your test scores." She looked at me strangely. "No, seriously. They said if you listen to Mozart while you're studying, your math scores can go up ten points. It's because it's so organized or logical or mathematical. They proved it. It really works. We could try it now. There's time. You want to?"

"You're going to play the cello?"

"That'd probably make you go down ten points," I said.

"Am I supposed to bark now?" she said.

I ignored that. "Besides, Mozart didn't write anything for cello. You must have some Mozart CDs, right, or tapes, or even records. And if we do it more than once . . ." Florence had two long shelves of music, but I couldn't remember what she had. "Come on." I pushed my chair back and stood up. "Let's go see."

"What if this doesn't work?" she said, when we got to the living room. I rummaged through CDs and she squatted down to look at album covers. *"Phantom of the Opera,"* she read out. "The Beatles . . . I don't see any Mozart."

"Keep looking. We'll find something. Look, here's *Beethoven's Greatest Hits.* Beethoven might be okay."

"What are you looking for?" a voice said. I jumped. David was standing in the doorway, barefoot, wearing his shredded jeans and a faded flannel shirt, half buttoned. His hair was wet and tangled from the shower. He was looking at me. Not smiling, just looking. I'd worn something nicer than usual that day, a long skirt and my sister's velvet vest and her white blouse, because I wanted to look more musicianlike for the conservatory. Now I thought he might be wondering why I was dressed up.

Emily stood up and explained what we were doing. "You don't see any Mozart there?" he said. I shook my head, but before I could say anything else, he left.

"Let's forget it," Emily said. "Let's just go to my room."

But a minute later, he was back, carrying his guitar. "Does it have to be Mozart?" he said. He shoved aside the books and magazines on the coffee table, sat down, crossed one leg over his knee, and, without another word, began to play. I don't know what I was expecting—"Rudolph" again maybe, or some folk song. Definitely not what I was hearing.

"What are you doing?" Emily said.

"Math music," he said. Then to me, "You think this might work?" meeting my eyes just long enough to see that I recognized what he was playing.

But I'm so cool, I said it anyway. "That's a cello piece," I said. "That's the first Bach unaccompanied cello suite." I thought that might earn me another of his *duhs*, but instead he gave me a small nod and kept on playing.

"*You're* going to play for us?" Emily said.

"Why not?" he said. "I'm not doing anything else."

There's this thing when, even if someone's not look-ing at you, you know they're really aware of you. It hasn't happened to me that many times. I felt it with Angel the first time he took me up in the elevator. I definitely felt it now. "This is great, Emily," I said. "What do you think? Don't you think Bach might be really good?"

"You said Mozart," Emily said. "You said it needed to be Mozart."

"No, Bach is perfect," I said. "It's much more logical and mathematical than Mozart. Go get your math stuff." She left and came back with her binder and her books. He'd started the second movement now. I loved the way it sounded on the guitar, the way his left hand shaped the chords as the fingers of his right hand skimmed across the strings. It looked so easy. Of course, with the guitar you don't have a bow to worry about, and it's the bow that's the killer, but David was good.

"Do you go to the New York Conservatory?" I asked.

"Uh-uh," he said. "I used to take lessons at Juilliard. You know, the Pre-College. But I couldn't deal with it. Now I go somewhere else."

"How come?" Juilliard was the best.

"A lot of reasons." He finished the second movement and began the third.

"You know the whole suite?" I said.

"You must, too, right? Every cellist plays the suites."

I didn't, but I didn't tell him. I'd learn them. I could go to Patelson's and get the music. I sat down on the floor about six feet from him and arranged my skirt around my legs.

"Hey. I thought we were going to study," Emily said.

"We are," I said. "We'll start right now."

"So what exactly am I supposed to do?" she said.

"I don't know," I said. "There weren't, like, instructions. Read through your notes, I guess. Try some problems. Don't focus on the music, just let it percolate." She sat down next to me. I checked my watch. "Okay, it's ten-forty."

David went back to the beginning and this time played the whole suite through. I liked it even better than the first time. For most of it, he had his eyes closed, which could be how he always played. But it may have been because I was staring at him. Not purposely. I never intend to stare at people. But I kept looking at his wrists, which were thin and covered with fine reddish hairs, and at his hands. Guitarist's hands. I was trying to see if guitarists got those knobby calluses like Miss Hauptman's, but his fingers moved too fast. I was also trying to decide what kind of animal he was. Most people, if you study them long enough, look like animals. Emily is an antelope. Florence, as we know, is a buffalo. My English teacher looks like a hedgehog. And my sister insists I look like a llama. "But only when you're mad," she says, as if that makes it okay. But I looked and looked at David and couldn't pin him down.

When he finished the Bach, he switched to something I'd never heard, something that made me think of Gypsies and ruined castles and a proud, solitary nobleman on horseback. But how do you describe how music sounds? How do you get words to say how something makes you feel? I mean, I can say it was in a minor key. And that it was so beautiful I felt it in my throat. But if I try to say the notes rippled like water or shimmered like leaves in the wind, I just seem corny and pretentious. Which is what usually bothers me about the poems I write. And which is why I love music in the first place.

David loved it, too. I could tell by the curve of his neck, by the way his fingers moved over the strings. But then Emily said, "Hey, guys. I've gone over everything three times. If it hasn't worked now, it's never going to."

"That wasn't Bach. What was that?" I said, as David put down the guitar, stood up, and stretched.

"Rodrigo," he said. "Nice, huh? I don't know if it's math music . . ."

"Who cares," I said. "It's really beautiful."

"Yeah, but what if it doesn't work?" Emily said.

"It'll work," I told her. "You're really good," I said to David. "Do you know if Rodrigo wrote anything for cello?"

"I don't know," he said. Then he stood up, picked up his guitar, and left.

"How good do you think you have to be," I asked

Emily as soon as he was gone, "to, like, make the leap from just some person who takes cello lessons to *cellist?* So, like, if you meet someone you can say, 'Hi, I'm Sarah. I'm a cellist.' "

"Why couldn't you say that now?" she asked. "You just said your teacher told you you had cellist's hands. Aren't you going to check my answers?"

"Oh. Sure." I took her workbook over to the coffee table and forced myself to focus, but I kept finding myself looking down the hall toward David's room.

We went over the first problem. It was right. So was the next one, and the next. She missed only four out of twenty. "I don't believe this," she said. "It's a miracle!"

"I believe it! You passed!" I cried, a lot louder than I really needed to, hoping David would hear it and come out.

"So you were right about the Bach," she said, looking more pleased with herself than I'd ever seen her.

"Hey, it wasn't Bach," I said. "It was you. You did it. Bach was the accompaniment. Face it." I thumped her on the shoulder. "We're great. You get us started, there's no stopping us."

It was time to go, and David hadn't reappeared. I stalled as long as I could, putting on my jacket, but I was at the door when he finally came out, muttering something about an English muffin. "Leaving?" he said. I nodded. "You be back next week or sometime?"

My heart gave a bump. "I don't know." I looked at Emily. "Yeah, I guess. Maybe."

" 'Cause I was thinking about what you said, about if Rodrigo wrote anything for cello." He raked his fingers through his hair, which had dried into these long, frizzy sort of curlicues. "I was thinking it'd be interesting to hear it if he did."

Chapter 4

My brain was still fizzing when I reached the conservatory. David's words kept bouncing in my head: "Every cellist plays the suites."

I got to the room before Miss Hauptman, so after I'd unpacked and tuned, I tried the Bach. I played the first few measures from memory, which was pretty good, I thought, considering I'd heard it dozens of times but had never seen the music. I'd been fooling around with it a few minutes when the door opened.

"Better try that again," Miss Hauptman said. She was wearing the same black suit, this time with a large silver cat pin with yellow jewels for eyes. Her own eyes were brown and glinted as brightly as the cat's. "You don't need nearly that much bow to get across the strings."

"I was just fooling around," I said, suddenly even more nervous than last week. "I've never learned this. I just heard someone playing it on the guitar today—"

"It doesn't matter," she said. "There's no point playing it wrong. These are dances, not exercises. Have you listened to Casals?" Pablo Casals was probably the greatest cellist of all time. Luckily, the first CDs I'd bought were of him playing all six suites, which was why I could play the beginning from memory. I nodded. "Then you know. You also know that you never want that accent at the beginning of each measure." She bent over to pick up her cello. "Not *blah* da *da* da *da* da *da* da . . ." She sang the first measure the way I'd just played it. I was glad her back was to me so she couldn't see my face.

"Why do you suppose you're getting that accent?" she said when she'd come back with the cello and sat down next to me.

"I'm not sure." I wished I'd never started this.

"Analyze it."

"Because I have zero control of my bow?"

She tightened her own bow. "I wouldn't have put it quite that way." She checked her tuning and adjusted her D string. "Though it has everything to do with your bow arm. Look. Watch my arm. Watch carefully how I do it." She played the first few lines, explaining as she played. I was glad to sit back and watch: (a) she was so good it was like sitting next to Casals; (b) it got the focus off me. "I'd like to start you on the left hand first," she said when she put down her bow.

"You're going to let me work on this?" I said, thinking of David, itching now to try it for myself.

"Isn't that what you had in mind?" When she smiled

her eyes softened, but they still had that glint. "You mentioned you heard someone play it on the guitar." I nodded. "That's a good way to approach this piece, strumming the chords. Why don't you . . ."

I started to play the first measure pizzicato, which is to say, plucking the strings instead of bowing.

"Excuse me!" she said. The dread excuse me, beloved by teachers the world over.

I froze.

"I was talking," she said, "and you played right over me." I apologized. "How do you expect to learn anything if you're too impatient to find out what I was going to say. Unless, that is, you already know everything there is to know." I apologized again. "Enthusiasm is fine. I like your enthusiasm. But you'll have plenty of time to play these suites. Believe me, Sarah, if you stick with the cello, you'll be working on these suites for the rest of your life." She pulled a pile of music from her canvas bag and leafed through it till she found the Bach. "Here," she said, putting it on the stand and smoothing it open to the first prelude. Her voice still had an edge. "*Now* you can try it."

We spent the entire lesson on the prelude, most of it strumming, which felt totally awkward, and a little working on the bow, which felt even worse because she corrected everything I did. But I didn't interrupt again and she went on as if nothing had happened, either not noticing or not caring that I was having a bad time. It was a relief when the next student arrived for her lesson.

"By the way," Miss Hauptman said after she'd greeted Natalie, who dressed in black and wore glasses and was clearly very good, "don't think, because every week I don't hear everything you've prepared, that I've forgotten any of it. That includes your scales."

"I practiced them a lot," I said, brave again now that my bow was loosened and my end pin pushed in. "I practiced everything a lot."

"I'm sure you did," she said. "We'll hear the first Popper étude next week." She picked up her cello and reviewed the problems in the étude for me. "If you master all of it, feel free to look over number two."

I left there too grouchy to go to Patelson's, and I stayed grouchy the whole next week. That thing she said, "if you stick with the cello," irked me so much I learned not just the prelude, but the whole first suite. But I hated the stupid strumming and I hated how I sounded. I hated it even more after I listened to Casals. "Listen to me," I yelled at anyone around. "I can't play this for David! I can't play anything! *Blah* da *da* da *da* da *da* da!" Singing the Bach the way I sounded, the way Miss Hauptman had imitated me, like a dancing elephant. "How could I think I was a cellist? Why am I even doing this?"

By the end of the week, even Saint Shelley the Nice was so sick of me my mother told me to go upstairs and practice in my room.

It didn't help that I couldn't go over to the Friedmans' that Saturday. Emily got an eighty-two on that math test, the best score she'd ever gotten, and her father was so ecstatic he was taking her to the Ice Capades. I knew I was supposed to be excited for her. But all I could think was, what if she has a good time and starts spending all her Saturdays with her father? Then I'd never see David.

It sleeted the day of my next lesson. The sky was gray. The slush was gray. I wore my old mud-colored corduroys and an unmusician-like gray sweatshirt. Miss Hauptman was wearing guess what: the black suit, with a silver dachshund on the collar.

"I am totally discouraged," I said when I played my scale for her. "I worked and worked and listen to me. I'm getting worse. I can't even play a scale."

"That's no surprise." She smiled. "It's what we call the rude awakening. It's happening somewhat faster with you than with some students, but it always happens. It's part of the process. You're learning to hear differently. You're hearing things you never heard before."

"How terrible I am, you mean."

No smile now. No sympathy, either. "If you like the way you sound, you'll never get better."

We started the Popper. "See!" I said when she immediately stopped me. "This is why I'm so frustrated. At home, I got this. Now I've lost it. You put something together and it falls apart."

"Exactly. And you keep working and eventually it comes together again at a slightly higher level. You notice I said slightly."

Or maybe that happened at a different lesson. There were a few weeks that sort of blur together now, when I sounded horrible and everyone, including me, was fed up with my bad temper, and it seemed to sleet constantly and Emily had the flu so I couldn't visit.

One afternoon, after a particularly dreary day at school, I called Emily.

David answered. It was the first time that had ever happened.

"Is this Sarah?" he said. My stomach leapt. "What's up?"

"Nothing much," I said. "What about you?"

"*Nada.*"

My throat was suddenly so dry, I drank from the glass on my bedside table, forgetting the water had been there for a week. "You didn't get the flu?"

"Not yet."

"So, how's the guitar?"

"Same old, same old."

"This conversation isn't going too well," I said.

"Well, how's the cello?"

"Fine," I said. Then I figured, why not tell him? "Actually, I feel like throwing it out the window." He laughed. "I'm serious."

"What floor are you on?"

I was up in my room, but for some reason I said, "The basement."

"Then it probably isn't worth it."

"I get so frustrated. I wish there were some, like, valve I could open and it would let the music come out the way it sounds in my head."

He laughed again. "I feel like that constantly."

"You?" I said.

"Yeah, all the time." Neither one of us said anything for a moment. Then he said, "Remember how you liked that thing I played?"

"The Rodrigo. Yeah."

"Well, there's no cello version." Which meant he'd checked. My breath caught. "But I was listening to the radio the other night. It was, like, three A.M., and they were playing this cello thing and it was really cool and I started remembering you liked the Rodrigo and I thought, Sarah needs to hear this. You probably already know it. It's probably, like, the most famous cello piece in history and you've been playing it your whole life . . ."

"What was it?"

"I think they said 'Song of the Birds.' "

"I don't know it," I said. "I'd like to hear it . . ."

"Well, maybe I can find it somewhere. And then next time you're over, I'll play it for you."

I could feel the sweat pop out on my hands, but I said, "Cool."

Chapter 5

It was easy getting Emily to invite me over. What was hard was waiting until Saturday. Then I almost missed my train from changing my clothes so many times, trying to decide between all black, like Miss Hauptman, or flannel, like David, or my mother's "more appropriate" choice, which I got stuck with, because she was out in the car, honking.

When I got to the Friedmans', I walked smack into a Florence cleaning rampage. "Look at this place!" she was shouting, her face redder than her fuchsia sweatsuit. She'd turned the vacuum off for one minute to greet me, but now she was roaring around with it again. "Who left this mess? Who's strewing nasty tissues everywhere?"

"I only see one," Emily said. "You're the one with the cold, so it must be yours. We're going to my room."

I could hardly believe Emily was talking like that, but Florence's eyes—which at the best of times look somewhat googly because of her glasses—were about to pop out of her head. "You pick it up this instant!" she ordered. "And David! Do something about your magazines."

David had come out practically as soon as I arrived, but we'd had no chance to say anything to each other. He grabbed a pile of books and magazines from the chair and started to walk away, too, but Florence said, "Not so fast. Isn't anybody going to give me some help around here?"

"What do you need?" I said.

"For someone to pick up the laundry, for one. Emily? Sweetheart?" Emily was the laundry lady.

"I brought it down," Emily said.

"Yes. And now it's ready to be brought back up."

"Why me?" Emily's jaw was set. "I always do it."

"Why don't I go?" I said. "It'll only take five minutes."

"I'll come with you," David said.

"That's a first," said Florence.

"Yeah, well, I'm feeling helpful," David said.

My heart began galloping as Florence handed him the laundry basket. Then we were in the hall, alone. David rang for the elevator. "What's her problem?" I said, hoping my voice sounded okay.

"Dinner party. Florence always goes berserk when there're people coming for dinner. Basement please," he told the elderly elevator man as the door opened. For the first time, I didn't miss Angel not being there. "She's also pissed she's lost her doormat."

"Huh?" I said.

"Emily. You didn't notice?" Now he looked at me. "Mommy's perfect little Emily has started talking back."

"But that's good," I said.

"For Emily, yeah. It's about time. But try telling that to Florence."

Then we were in the basement, walking down this long, empty corridor to the laundry room—this big, echoey, cement-floored place with rows of thumping dryers and clanking washing machines, big ancient sinks, pipes running all across the ceiling, and a strong smell of disinfectant. We were all alone. "I hate it down here," I said. We went over and found the two dryers with the Friedmans' stuff, pulled everything out, and piled it on the table. "It reminds me of a morgue."

"Why?" He pulled an orange towel from the tangle and folded it.

"It just does," I said.

"I always think of morgues as cold," he said. "It's hot in here."

"That's true," I said. I pulled out a very large pair of nylon underpants and folded them in half. They still looked pretty big, so I folded them again. "Could be because it's next to the boiler room." That seemed to be a conversation stopper. I folded all of Florence's underwear and started on Emily's white cotton panties. Twelve pairs, I counted. I wasn't that happy dealing with people's underwear, though, so I switched to socks. I could feel David watching as I arranged them in an even row. The fluorescent lights flickered on the pale-green tiled walls.

"It's the light," I said. "You have to admit, the light in here is morguelike."

"You ever go to the whale hall in the Museum of Natural History?" He'd finished the towels and was on to T-shirts.

"Not since, like, the second grade." I noticed that the fingernails on his right hand were long, for plucking the guitar strings, but the left-hand nails were bitten.

"Did you go downstairs to where they have the underwater scenes? That's what the light in here reminds me of."

"I think it's the bulbs," I said, rolling the socks into the neatest balls known to man. "They need to change the bulbs. You don't call it a bulb though, do you, when it's, like, fluorescent. What is it?"

"A tube. It's a cool place, the fish hall. You should go there sometime."

"I'll check it out," I said.

"I go there a lot. It's not like I'm a fish fanatic or anything. I just like it there. Like, when I'm really bummed, or have a lot on my mind, I go there and hang out."

"By yourself?" I said.

"Does that sound weird?"

I shook my head. "Not really. I have a place like that. Or I used to. Till my dad pruned it into extinction."

"A tree?"

"A bush, actually." I hesitated, then thought, oh go ahead. "A rhododendron."

"Cool."

I looked at him more closely. "You know what that is?"

"Sure. My aunt has one next to the house. They have, like, big puffy purple flowers, right?"

"What are you doing?" I said. He was taking one of Florence's black-and-purple-flowered king-sized sheets, opening it out partway, then sort of rolling it into a lump.

"Folding the sheets," he said.

"That's not folding," I said. "That's called crunching. Haven't you ever folded laundry?"

"Yeah. This is how I do it."

"And I bet Florence loves it." I opened out the sheet until I found two corners.

"You're ruining my nice work," he said.

"I'm just showing you. See, I take these two corners. You hold the other ones." He did and I backed up till the whole sheet was opened out. "David!" I'd never called him by his name before. It seemed to hang there in the air. "Hold it up! You don't want to drag it on the ground." He made a goofy face. I laughed. "Now, we sort of flap it around to get rid of the wrinkles." He gave a mighty yank. "Not that hard!" He laughed. "Now fold it in half lengthwise. Good. Now turn it flat." I moved toward him.

We were standing very close together now, and as he handed me his corners, his fingers brushed lightly against mine. I was suddenly all electrified and jittery, like I'd had eighteen cups of coffee. I stepped back. We did another fold. My throat was tight from trying not to giggle. "And now I give you these two ends." Our hands touched again. Then we made one last fold, and it was done. "You never did this before?" I said. We were still standing so close together, I felt compelled to say something.

"Possibly." He put the folded sheet into the laundry basket, then turned back to me. "It wasn't one of the high points of my life."

I picked up the other sheet. "Okay," I said. "Now this one is a fitted sheet, with these bunchy corners." Shut up, Sarah, I told myself as he took his corners and stepped away from me. He knows what a fitted sheet is. "A fitted sheet is much harder to make into a neat package." We moved together till our bodies were almost touching and, once again, our fingers brushed. "You realize this is vital information I'm giving you," I said. "Laundry lessons. Highly educational."

"Does anyone really care?" His words were flip, but he was looking right into my eyes, and his eyes were warm. "So I don't even know where you live," he said. Definitely warm. "Where *do* you live, Long Gyland?"

"Unfortunately."

"It stinks?"

"Not for some people. My sister likes it." We'd finished folding everything, but we were still standing there. I started worrying that he could hear me breathe. I straightened the edges on my pile of underwear.

"So I guess you're glad you come in for lessons Saturdays."

I nodded. When people nod their heads, they usually do it about two or three times. My head started nodding and it didn't stop.

He was still looking right into my eyes.

"We should go back up," I said. "Emily's waiting for me. For the math. I promised her we'd do math again." I waited for him to offer to play for us again, but he didn't.

We were back in the elevator before I dared ask, "Did you ever find that piece you mentioned? 'Song of the Birds?' "

"I meant to go down and look for it at Tower Records. I was going to check their computer—"

"It's okay," I said.

"No," he said. "I'll go Monday. I want you to hear it." That "you" felt even more personal than when he touched me. And when we reached the apartment, before he put his key in the door, he added, "Unless you want to meet me there next Saturday. Then after, we can go to the museum and check out my old friends, the fish."

Emily was right there waiting when we went in. "That took you long enough," she said.

"Sorry," I said. "There was a lot of laundry."

"Sarah had to give me laundry lessons," David said.

I tried to make my face look serious, or at least normal.

"Now there's no time to work on my math," she said.

"There's lots of time." I looked at my watch. "My lesson's not till twelve. I don't have to leave till quarter of.

Plus," I said, "I just thought it would be better to fold the stuff down there so it wouldn't get all wrinkly."

"Sarah! Sweetheart!" Florence burst forth from the kitchen, drying her hands on a paper towel. "You're a truly wonderful human being. Thank you so much! How do I ever survive in this place without you?"

"What about me?" David said. "Don't I get thanked?"

"After you tie up all the newspapers and take them to the basement."

He made a face, but he followed Florence to the kitchen, and Emily and I went to her room. I wasn't sure if I should say anything to her about David, but out it blurted before she'd even closed her door. "I think he may have asked me out!" I said. "He wants me to meet him at Tower Records next week."

She went to her desk and got her math books and her notebook and lay down on the floor. "It's conversions," she said. "They're even worse than inequalities."

I sat down next to her. "I think I want to go."

"Duh," she said.

"It's that obvious?"

She opened her notebook to a clean page and wrote a heading. "I'm not completely blind."

"Have I done anything embarrassing?" I said. "Am I acting ridiculous?"

She put a row of numbers in the margin. "It's not just you."

"Emily!" I swatted her. "Seriously. I'm not, am I?" Though I was thinking, *He likes me! She sees it, so it must be true!* "He seems like a really great guy," I said, wanting to hear more about him, wanting to know everything about his life.

She snorted. "That's what everyone *thinks*."

"What does that mean?"

"Nothing." She suddenly had a closed-off, distant look that reminded me of when I'd first met her.

"C'mon, tell me." I tried to make a joke of it. "Emily, you're not jealous?"

"Why would I be jealous? I'm not jealous. I just think you should know what you're getting into with him."

"I'm not getting into anything. Necessarily. We don't even have a date yet. He probably won't even call."

"Don't worry," she said. "I know how David is. He'll call."

Chapter 6

"Do you know something called 'Song of the Birds?' "
I asked Miss Hauptman. She was in the middle of showing me a bow stroke, but my brain was *boing*ing, bur-
bling, bubbling over, and my fingers were still tingling
from David's touch.

She stopped playing. "Why do you ask?"

"Just, this person I know mentioned it." I didn't want
to upset Emily. I really didn't. But the whole way over
here, I'd thought about my life—my predictable, bland,
boring Long Island life—and something told me if he did
call, I would go.

Miss Hauptman's eyebrows went up ever so slightly. "I
see," she said. She played a few measures of something
slow and sad. It had the same minor, Spanish sound as
the Rodrigo he had played for me.

"Is that it?" I said.

She nodded. "It's an old Catalan folk song. Casals arranged it for the cello."

"It's nice," I said.

"Oh, it's more than nice," she said.

She began to play again. It started quietly, just this simple melody, like someone singing to herself. Then, slowly, the sound warmed and deepened and it began to build, until it swelled into a fierce, soaring, shining anthem. Sad and happy both. I felt like she was singing about something I had lost, only I couldn't remember what it was.

I would have loved this piece even if it wasn't David who told me about it, but as she played, I thought of him lying in his bed late at night, listening, feeling those same feelings, and thinking about me.

"I have to play that," I said.

She put her bow down on the stand and smiled. "You will," she said. "I played it with Casals, you know. At Prades. I was part of a whole cello orchestra. I wish I had a recording of it to play for you."

"I want to play like that," I said.

"We all want to play like that," Miss Hauptman said.

"No," I said. "No. I meant, like you. Like you just played. I want to sound like that."

My words vibrated in the air. My throat tightened. I felt as if I'd just looked down and noticed I had nothing on.

But Miss Hauptman smiled. That's not quite accurate.

Her mouth smiled, and the creases all around her eyes softened, but the eyes themselves seemed to sharpen. Like my cat's when he's spotted a grasshopper in the lawn. "Well, my dear," she said, pronouncing it *muh-dear*, looking friendlier than I'd ever seen her, but at the same time, definitely formidable. "Then we'd better get to work."

By the end of the lesson, my arms ached, my fingertips were sore, and sweat trickled down inside my shirt. And when I got home, I ignored the rule of life which states you never practice the evening of your lesson, and I worked some more.

I'd bought "Song of the Birds" on my way to the train. I was learning the notes when the phone rang.

"You still want to do something next Saturday?" David said. "I'll meet you at the conservatory after your lesson."

"Sure," I said. Maybe Emily wouldn't mind.

The week crawled by. All I really did, besides think about Saturday, was practice: half an hour of scales and exercises when I got home from school, an hour of Bach and Popper after dinner, and at least another half hour on "Song of the Birds."

By Saturday, something in my playing had changed. I heard it and Miss Hauptman heard it, and she worked me even harder than the week before. "Again," she kept demanding, "try it again," as she circled around me, adjusting this and poking that, shoving my left hand, steering my bow arm. By halfway through the lesson, I was wiped out. "Push yourself, Sarah," she said, as I fought the urge to slump down in my seat. "Focus. The cello can't do it. You have to do it."

"There's so much to learn," I moaned.

"Don't worry," she said. "You just keep working. I'll teach you."

David was waiting for me when I reached the lobby. "We don't need to go to Tower Records," I blurted the instant he smiled at me. "I got 'Song of the Birds.' My teacher played it for me." I liked the sound of that: *my teacher*. "I love it. I've already learned it."

"Great," he said. "We'll go straight to the museum. I'll carry the cello." Without waiting for my answer, he lifted the strap and hoisted it to his shoulder.

It was extremely cold out, with one of those winds that makes your eyes tear and stings the inside of your nose. We started downtown, walking fast, hunched over, hardly talking. David had on a leather jacket that didn't look warm enough at all, and a maroon scarf but no gloves. My ears felt ready to snap off, but I resisted putting on my hood, since that would permanently squash my hair.

When we got to the museum, he showed his pass and we headed down a wide corridor full of little kids and foreign tourists and old ladies and daddies pushing stroll-

ers, all looking at the glassed-in miniature replicas of
farms and life-sized forest scenes and other nature stuff.
I've always been really interested in nature stuff, but
David kept on going, past a giant redwood and a wild
turkey and a great display called "Life of the Forest
Floor," which had a five-foot millipede and a two-foot
acorn and a humongous daddy longlegs. "Oh, cool!" I
said. "Let's stop."

"On the way back," he said. "I'm taking you to the
fish."

Finally we stepped through a passageway that opened
into a dark, enormous hall. The light was dim, greenish,
and flickery. It was like being underwater. Ahead of us,
suspended from the ceiling, loomed the Great Blue
Whale. We walked over to a flight of stairs, which led
down to another hall below the whale. There were people wandering all around, but it was so silent it felt as if
we were alone.

"Well, here we are," he said, looking at me so intently
my heart, which had finally begun acting normal, started
to race again. "What do you think?"

"Reminds me of your laundry room," I said. "Same
ambiance."

"No, seriously." He nodded toward the far wall, where
life-sized sharks and swordfish and giant skates swam
against a pale green background. "What I never get is,
everybody comes to see the whale and they totally ignore
the other stuff. I mean, look at them. They look so alive,

like they're just swimming along, minding their business—"

I pointed to a pudgy kid in a red snowsuit. "Waiting for some tasty morsel to happen by."

"Go ahead, mock me," David said. "I like the sharks. Sharks are my friends."

I was about to make a reference to Florence, when a short, gray-haired, African-American lady in a guard uniform came up next to us. "What's that you've got there, Davey, a machine gun?" She had a lilting accent and lively eyes. But Davey? I couldn't imagine calling David Davey.

"It's a cello," David said.

"Why didn't you tell me you played the cello? Keeping secrets from me, eh?" She winked at me.

"It's Sarah's," he said. "Sarah, this is Althea." I said hi.

"Yeah, he's in here all the time," Althea said, looking me over, "but always by himself. I tease him about when's he going to find himself a new young lady."

"Thanks, Althea," David said. His face was getting redder by the minute. "You're a real pal."

"Uh-oh, look at this," she said. "I didn't mean to make him blush." By this time I was blushing, too. "You want to leave that cello with me? I'll put it in the closet so no one will bother it and you can walk around."

We left the cello with Althea and went downstairs, where it was even quieter and the light was even dimmer and more flickery. We stopped in front of every scene:

the coral reefs with the pearl divers, the stuffed walrus, the electric eels; but David didn't say anything. I had the urge to say, "You sure have clammed up," but so far my attempts to make him laugh had come out either lame or strange. Finally he nodded toward a bench and said, "Want to sit down?"

We sat, but fairly far apart.

"She seems nice, Althea," I said after a bit.

"She's not usually so embarrassing. I worked here last year, for my service credit. That's how come I know her. She used to share her sandwich with me. It's a really boring job being a guard, so she got to hear my whole life story."

It occurred to me that she probably knew more about David than I did. "I don't even know what school you go to," I said.

He told me the name. "It's a private school."

"You like it there?"

He shrugged. "I go, I do what I have to do, I come home. Anyway, a few months ago, when I was so bummed out, I started hanging out here again."

"I can see why," I said. "It's great here."

"You think so?" He suddenly looked like he was six years old.

"Uh-huh." I had this surge of feelings. "I'm really glad we came."

That *we* seemed to shimmer in the air.

"You're wondering what she meant, though, 'new young lady,' right? I was watching you. I saw you wondering." He wasn't even looking at me, but I felt like I could hardly breathe. "There was this . . . person I used to—"

"I know," I said, not looking at him, either. "I heard. I'm sorry."

"Yeah, well . . ." I thought he might be mad that Emily had told me, but he took my hand. "Anyway, I'm over her." He started playing with my fingers, sort of fiddling with them one by one.

"What're you doing," I said, "playing This Little Piggy?"

He laughed. It was a relief to hear him laugh. "I don't know. Just looking at them."

"Can you feel my callouses? I'm practicing a lot."

He rubbed his finger lightly on my fingertips. "Sorry. You better practice more."

"Feel again."

He did. "Okay, maybe a tiny callous. You still better practice more."

He was stroking his thumb across my palm now, which sent my blood whirring through my veins. "I always used to hate my hands," I said, "but Miss Hauptman said they're cellist's hands. She told me that when I went to audition for her."

"I don't know about your hands," he said, "but you definitely have cellist's eyebrows."

I giggled. "What's that supposed to mean?"

"You're going to make me figure out what I mean

again?" He scrutinized my face. "They're, like, I don't know, very serious and intense."

"And they vibrate on the low notes?" He laughed. "My sister thinks I should pluck them."

"Don't," he said. "I like them."

"I hope you realize I just made a pun," I said. "Cello? Plucked? Pizzicato?"

"I was trying to ignore it," he said. "Can I tell you something? I was a little nervous about today. Being with you, you know?" He wasn't looking at my eyebrows now. It felt like he was staring at my mouth. He moved closer.

"I was nervous, too," I said. "I'm a little nervous now." I was dying to wipe my hand on my jeans, but I didn't know if I'd have the guts to take his hand again. "You can tell by how much I'm talking. Plus, I wouldn't have made that stupid pun if I wasn't nervous."

No question. He was staring at my lips. He was going to kiss me in front of the walrus and a bunch of babies and a Cub Scout troop.

I hadn't done much kissing at that point. I'd watched plenty of other people, notably my sister and her inane boyfriend, Bart. When I was, like, twelve and starting to go to parties, I practiced on my drinking glass, until my sister blabbed out, right at the breakfast table, "Sarah's kissing her juice!" I told them my lip itched, but not even she believed me. The first person who kissed me was at one of those parties. It was Jeffrey Gerber, a.k.a. the Gerber Baby, a.k.a. Jeffrey the Gerbil, and I didn't kiss him back. I did kiss this other person, Jason, back, but he was such a space cadet, I don't think he knew the difference.

David knew the difference. He leaned very close to me. When his mouth was so close to mine I stopped breathing, he said, very softly, "So we're both nervous."

Chapter 7

"He kissed you?" My sister stopped brushing her hair and plunked herself beside me on my bed. "On the lips?"

I nodded. Ever since I'd gotten interested in David, Shelley had been more interested in me. I resented that it took my going out with someone for her to see me as a member of the human race. But I must admit, I was starting to like her showing up at bedtime in her night-gown, carrying her hairbrush or her toothbrush or her nail polish. Especially because I felt funny talking about him to Emily.

"So are you going to see him next Saturday, too?"

I nodded again.

"Sarah, this is so exciting!" She lay back and folded my pillow under her head. "So how many times did he kiss you?"

"Once," I said. She raised her eyebrows. "Okay.

Twice, but the second time was at Penn Station—I did tell you he went downtown on the subway with me when I went to get the train, right?—and it was only like, a little peck."

"Which means the first one must have been a major smooch."

"Shelley!" I grabbed the pillow from under her head and whomped her with it.

"This is just so cool." She sat up and smoothed her hair back to its previous perfection. "You've got a New York City boyfriend." Her eyes narrowed as she looked me over. "Want to know something? I think you even look a little different."

"You're crazy," I said. But when I got to school Monday, I felt different. Not my usual weird-different, like I'd just landed from another planet. Different-special, the way I felt in New York, carrying my cello case. I no longer walked around the halls seeing all the couples, thinking it would never happen to me.

"Museum again?" I asked David when he picked me up after my next lesson. Without discussing it, we'd started walking in the same direction as the week before.

"Nope," he said. "I thought we'd try another kind of fish experience today. Sort of variations on a fishy theme. You hungry?" I nodded. "How'd the lesson go?"

"Intense," I said. "We worked on Bach today—the gigue from the first suite, and we started the bourrées from the third suite." The bigger news was she'd promised to start me on a concerto the next week, by some guy named Goltermann, but before I could ask David if he'd ever heard of him, he started in singing the bourrée. "You play those, too?" I said.

"Yup."

"Sounds like you've played everything," I said. We were walking so close together, I wondered if people passing by would think we were a couple.

"Hardly," he said. "But Bach's cool. I'm just starting the C minor lute suite."

"Oh, I love that," I said. "But it must be really hard. Bach is so hard. You look different today." He was wearing baggy chinos and the leather jacket and a Yankees cap, which made his hair puff out around his ears. His chin was red, as if he had just shaved.

"Good or bad?"

"I don't know. Different." I remembered that first time I'd heard him playing the funereal "Rudolph" through the wall. I thought about the Rodrigo he had played for me, and now the lute suite. "Less sort of C minor. More C major."

"Hey." He took my hand and looked at me. "Today I'm definitely C major."

That seemed to make both of us a little awkward, so we walked for a bit, still holding hands, smiling but not saying anything, till I said, "Can I ask you a question? When you're thinking about yourself, in your mind, do you, like, call yourself a guitarist or a guitar player?"

He shrugged. "I don't think that much about it. I just do it."

"Well, then, when Florence describes you to some-one—"

"I do my best to pretend it isn't happening. Why?"

"I don't know. It's just, I keep wondering how good you have to be before you can call yourself a *cellist*."

He stopped walking. His eyes darkened. "Not you, too!" he said.

"What are you talking about?" I said.

"You wanted to know why I switched from Juilliard? That's why. Who's the star of the hour? Who's the best? Who's the teacher's pet? Everyone's so hung up on la-bels. You should do it 'cause you want to do it. The rest is garbage!"

I was too startled to say anything. But a minute later, he stopped in front of a Japanese restaurant. "Ever have sushi?" he said, as if nothing had happened.

I had no idea what was going on, but I didn't dare protest. "Raw fish?"

"Good." He was smiling again. "I wanted to do some-thing you'd never done before." He held the door for me and we went into a small, narrow restaurant with a long, low counter. "Let's sit right here at the sushi bar."

I propped my cello on the chair beside me. The front of the counter had a covered glass partition, behind which was a whole array of unidentified squishy objects. "This looks pretty expensive," I said, trying to avoid looking at all the slabs of different colored, uncooked-looking fish. "I don't have much money."

"Don't worry," he said. "I'm loaded. I saw my dad last

night. You can tell how guilty he's feeling about the amount of time he's spending with me by how much money he hands over. It's the old guilt-o-meter. Well, I'm spending it on something educational, right?" His laugh still had that edge. "Your sushi education."

"I guess," I said.

A sign on the wall listed the day's specials: giant clam, salmon eggs, monkfish liver, squid. Shelley would have died.

"I hope you realize," I said, "that my only previous contact with a squid was when I came into my home-room class, which happens to be the bio lab, and found out the teacher had ordered two hundred and forty of them to dissect and left them out all night."

"Okay, we'll skip the squid." He said something in Japanese to the man behind the counter, who nodded gravely, finished slicing a chunk of fish the color of bloody meat, then laid out a thin black sheet of what David said was dried seaweed. "Don't worry." He patted my arm. "We're starting you out with the not-too-scary stuff."

I watched as the man spread the seaweed with a thin layer of gummy-looking rice. He laid on some items I couldn't see, which was probably just as well, then rolled the whole thing in a bamboo mat. When he unrolled the mat, the food was in a very neat, hot dog–sized tube, which he sliced. Then he stood the pieces, end up, on a wooden board.

I gulped. "They look cute," I said.

The man nodded again and made two more rolls with

some more unknown items. After that, he formed rice into little blocks, which he topped with who knows what and bound with strips of seaweed, like bite-sized packages. Then he garnished the board with some artistically placed sprigs and passed it to us.

"It looks nice, right?" David said.

"Way too nice to eat," I said.

"Scaredy-cat," he said. "Try this one first." He pointed to a rice package with something brown on top. "It isn't squid. I promise."

"What is it?"

"That's for me to know and you to find out." I punched him. Still smiling, he picked one up with his chopsticks and popped it in his mouth. "Come on," he said after he'd swallowed. "Try it."

"I'm not great with chopsticks."

"Then use your fingers. But first, dip it in this." He poured some soy sauce into a tiny dish. "Mix in a little wasabi. That's this green blob here. Don't use a lot. Just this much." He mixed some in for me. "It's horseradish. It's hot."

I took a tiny bite and felt a pleasant stinging in my nose. "Okay. I'm still alive." I took a bigger bite. It didn't taste like fish at all. "This is actually good," I said.

"See, I know all about you. I knew you'd like it." He sat up straighter. "You're just like me." He looked incredibly pleased. "Have another one. This little guy here looks good."

I wish I could explain what it feels like when somebody

is usually so moody, almost melancholy, then suddenly he's transformed, and you think, ooh, hey, I did that! He looks like that because of me. It's a powerful, great, giddy feeling. David must have seen me feeling it, because his eyes brightened even more.

"So, what is it?" I said. I ate another, wiped my mouth, then ate a third. Even the stern sushi chef smiled.

"Eel," David said.

"Eel? The long slithery kind? Like, electric eel? Like those humongous guys we saw in the museum?"

"Don't worry." He patted me. "It's cooked. Trust me."

"Trust you?" I said. "I'm going to kill you."

He laughed. "Come on. You liked it."

I had to admit, it was good—sort of sweet and, as I said, not fishy.

"Plus," he said, "you can't kill me till you try the tuna." He pointed to one of the little rolls.

"Hey, tuna fish?" I said. "No problem."

"This one's raw."

"I handled eel, didn't I?"

Not only did I handle tuna, I loved it, even when David told me it came from that alarming blood-red slab. It tasted more like some delicious meat than fish and it was great with the wasabi. I was getting really hooked on that wasabi. "By the way," he said, after I'd eaten four of our six tuna rolls, "you only call it tuna fish when it comes in the can. Should we order another round?"

"Why not?" I said.

Stuffed walruses and raw fish may not be everyone's

idea of romance, but it sure worked for me. Or maybe they put something in the wasabi. Anyway, we stayed there in the restaurant for two hours. Then we wandered over to Central Park and walked beside a frozen lake and I couldn't have cared less that everything looked bleak and dirty in the feeble February light. David had his arm around me, which didn't work that well with the cello bumping against my other side, but I didn't care about that, either.

Too soon, it was time to get the train.

"Don't go," David said. "We'll call and tell your mom to meet a later train." He wrapped his arm around my neck. "We'll find a movie, get something to eat." He pushed my hair back and put his lips against my ear. I felt like my whole insides were swelling up so I could hardly breathe.

"We just ate," I said.

"Who cares. I don't want you to leave."

He pulled me to him, and we kissed. One part of me worried that I smelled like fish, but the other part gave myself over to it totally.

"Stay," he said.

I didn't stay. It took a long time to find a phone because we stopped so many times to kiss, and then, when we finally found one that worked, there was no one at my house. I knew they wouldn't have let me stay anyway, but I didn't tell him that.

"Next week," I said. That's how sure I was he liked me.

Chapter 8

When I think now about those first weeks, the phrase that pops into my head is "dreamy bliss"—the name of a sundae David and I ordered in an ice cream shop. For the first time in my life, nothing got to me. Not school, which I floated through as if it had no relation to my real life, or my parents, even though they asked endless questions about him and made me come back from the city earlier than I'd have liked. My cello playing zoomed ahead. Miss Hauptman assumed it was her brilliant teaching, which no doubt was true for the technique part. But I knew that wasn't all it was. Technique couldn't explain why my sound had gotten so much larger, warmer, fuller.

"It's simple," my sister said. "Love inspires people. And you are definitely in love. It's, like, so obvious." She'd walked in while I was practicing and picked up this list I'd written during English instead of taking notes on

Moby Dick. " 'David Friedman: What I like about him,' " she read out loud. "Let's see now. 'Musical. Double exclamation point.' Okay, that makes sense."

"So glad you approve," I said. It was pretty clear Emily didn't approve. She wasn't calling very much and when I called her, she acted like she couldn't wait to get off the phone.

" 'Smart. Sensitive. Tall,' " Shelley read on. "That's good. I don't care for shrimpy guys. 'Ironic.' What does that mean?"

"You wouldn't understand."

" 'Lanky.' Do you mean, like, skinny?"

"Shut up, Shelley!"

" 'Funny. Strange.' There's nothing here about being hot. Is he?"

I whacked her. "None of your business!"

"He is! I knew it! Is he nice, too? You left out nice."

"Nice is boring," I said. The famous Bart was the very essence of Nice. "Nice is bland. Nice is 'Have a great da-ay!' If it was a food, it would be mayo. You could die of Nice and probably wouldn't even know it. It'd be like slowly drowning in a huge tank of rice pudding."

"I like rice pudding," Shelley said.

"What a surprise."

"I do."

"Yeah, well, I'll take wasabi any day."

David and I hadn't gone back to the Japanese restaurant, though. We went to coffee bars instead, and the ice cream·place, and the skating rink, and the Lincoln Cen-

ter Library, where we sat in the corner, sharing headphones and holding hands while we played each other
our favorite recordings. He also bought me a major pile
of CDs. So many CDs my parents started making com-
ments. "He just wants me to have all the same music he
has," I explained, not telling them he'd done it so that
when we listened, we could make believe we were together.

We talked on the phone most nights and I met him
every Saturday. I took the 10:14 train to the city. My
lesson was at noon, and afterward he'd be waiting for me.
Then we'd have four hours together. Too short, but perfect. It felt almost too good to be true.

Guess what?

I was practicing a double-stop exercise when the phone
rang. It was the middle of March by then. I remember,
because when I got home from school that day, I'd spotted the first tiny yellow crocuses poking up beside the
rhododendron. "Emily, hi!" I said.

"How've you been?" Her voice sounded tight.

"I'm good," I said.

"How's David?"

"Good," I said again, though it seemed liked a weird
thing to ask about her own brother. "I've been wanting to
talk to you."

"Well, you haven't been over here in five weeks."

"I meant to," I said. "I've been pretty busy, I guess."
There was a long silence. I heard static, which meant she
was on the cordless phone, then a rhythmic sort of

squeaking. "What are you doing? Are you on the exercise bike?" Florence always called it "that damn bike." Last summer, when Emily was literally pedaling for hours, Florence had the super haul it away and lock it in the basement. It was clearly back.

"Not really," Emily said. I knew she was.

"Is everything all right?" I asked, afraid she'd stopped eating again. Afraid, suddenly, it was because of me. "Are you okay?"

More silence, then she said, "I have to get glasses." I could hear her breathing. "I wasn't going to call you . . ."

"Why not?"

"Well, I mean, you're so busy . . ."

"Emily! You should have picked up the phone and said, 'Sarah, you jerk, where the hell are you?' Here I've been thinking *you* didn't want to talk to *me*. I'd have been glad."

"Really?" Silence. "That's what Dr. Kahn said, too. He's always after me to speak up." Dr. Kahn was her therapist. "Anyway . . ." The squeaks got faster. "Florence is taking me to get the glasses Saturday. I guess I was thinking if I went with you, I could at least get something I liked, instead of, like, purple-and-green spangled ones. But you're doing something with David, right?"

"Just in the afternoon," I said. "I can come in early. We'll go before my lesson."

She exhaled into the phone. "I'm going to the dentist in the morning."

I know that crawly, helpless feeling when you have to ask for something. It's especially bad when it's something you really need. So even as I saw my precious hours with David dwindling, I said, "Don't worry about it. You'd do it for me, right? I'll work it out."

"It's okay," I assured David on the phone that night. "How long can picking glasses take? An hour, hour and a half, max. We'll be really decisive. And we'll find some place nearby. Then, after Emily and I get back, you and I can be together."

"In front of Florence?" David said. "Do you have any idea how grotesque that would be? '*David, sweet*heart!' " He went into a perfect and only slightly exaggerated imitation of Florence. " 'Why didn't you *tell* me you two were an item?' "

"We don't have to meet in the apartment," I said. "You'll meet me somewhere else."

"She'll start doing our charts, working out our astral conjunctions or whatever they're called; next thing you know she'll be booking the Rainbow Room for our wedding . . ."

"David," I said, "why are you making this into a big thing? It's just part of one afternoon. I promised Emily. I haven't seen her in five weeks. Besides, you don't want her to come back with rhinestone-studded spectacles, do you?"

"Fine," he said. The famous Friedman *fine*, specially designed to make a saint feel like a bad dog. "I'll just give the tickets to someone else. If I can find someone."

"What tickets?" I said. "Tickets to what? David?"

"It doesn't matter now, does it?"

"David." I was getting this queasy feeling that somehow things had spiraled out of my control. "I didn't know. You didn't say anything."

"I wanted it to be a surprise."

My mind gets so churned up when I'm upset and mad that I have trouble afterward remembering exactly what was said. All I recall is that David said he might just use the tickets anyway and the hot aching in my chest when I got off the phone.

Shelley, love-life advisor extraordinaire, kept saying things like, "Don't worry. You said yourself he's sensitive. He's only acting like this because he really cares. He'll call back." And then, the next day, "Don't worry, he'll be there Saturday."

But by Saturday, when he still hadn't called, you can guess how I was feeling.

Chapter 9

My lesson started really badly. We slogged through the usual up-bow staccato scales and thumb position octaves and began the Goltermann. Within the first five minutes Miss Hauptman had told me to wake up, fix my intonation, count, concentrate, put some guts into it, and stop tickling the strings. That one really rankled.

"I had a rough week," I said.

"Yes," she said, not unkindly, but making it clear she wasn't interested in the details. She reached down to her bag and rummaged through her music. "Let's try something different," she said, finally selecting a thin, yellow book. She passed the music over to me—Handel G Minor Sonata for two cellos—and picked up her cello. "You'll take the second part," she said. "It's not hard. But," she said, looking at me severely, "you're going to have to pay attention, Sarah. That means count. And listen."

I nodded.

"Now sit up straight and let me hear your A." She tightened her bow and we compared our tuning. Then she talked me through some problems, wrote in some fingerings, and pointed out my solo. "I'm on my own for the first six measures." Her back was totally erect, her body completely still, her eyes almost closed. I could feel her gathering herself. "Now, ready: one, two, three, four . . ."

The instant she started playing, I was riveted. If you had the sensitivity of a clam, you'd have been riveted. So I came in right. My melody repeated hers: sweet and expressive, strong, and really stirring. She had to stop me a few times to get the dotted rhythms, but when I did get it, I got so excited, I did the unthinkable: I counted out loud. Which meant when there were some confusing rests, I didn't mess them up.

She looked at me and nodded, smiling. I smiled back. It was the first time I had smiled in days.

"Nice!" she said, when I tried to match the way she shaped a phrase. "Very nice!" she said when I leaned into my vibrato the exact same way she did.

I was flying.

The second movement was marked *allegro energico*, so I had to really scramble to keep up; but she pulled me along, supporting me through the high, fast passages, getting me to play better, play out. I totally amazed myself. "Did you hear that?" I said when we were through. "I couldn't do that last week. I'm improving!"

"I was just thinking the same thing," she said. She said it briskly as usual, but there was no question about the way she looked at me.

"I love this sonata," I said. "I love Handel." I loved her, too.

And I loved David. Shelley was right. It had to be because of him, because of loving him, that I could play like this.

"I think you should join my cello workshop," Miss Hauptman said, still smiling. "It meets the fourth Saturday of every month. Most of my students come. We get together and play for each other, whatever anyone is working on. It's not a performance. It's a working session, a way to iron out the wrinkles in your playing."

I nodded, but the details barely registered. I was too busy thinking about all the things I'd tell David, things that would sound stupid to anybody else. Like how I'd tried to match Miss Hauptman's sound, blend in, disappear inside the music until there was no me, only the music we were making. How I'd listened not just with my ears or with my brain, but with my entire body. How I felt as if I'd been waiting my whole life to do this and never known. How I felt as if anything was possible.

But then the door creaked open, and Natalie stuck her head in. "You may come in," Miss Hauptman said. "We're finished. I've just suggested to Sarah that she sit in at our next cello workshop." She was still giving me that wonderful new approving look.

Natalie, whom I'd seen every single week since January, stared at me now as if I were some new and possibly toxic life-form.

"Natalie's going to play the *Rococo Variations* for us," Miss Hauptman said as I packed. That was Tchaikovsky. Really hard. Totally intimidating. But I felt too happy to be intimidated. The whole fight with David suddenly seemed absurd. I couldn't wait to see him.

"Practice hard," Miss Hauptman said, as I opened the door to leave. "Hurry up and get that thumb in shape, so I can start you on a Boccherini. And don't forget to tell your parents about the cello group. It's officially three to five, but it usually runs longer. So tell them you might be home late next week."

Chapter 10

Next week? What was I going to do?

I walked to the Friedmans' as quickly as I could.

"Are you okay?" Emily asked. She'd been waiting on the front step of her building, peering down the street, but as I got near, her smile faded. "Do you still want to do this with me? Because if you don't—"

"No, I do," I said. "I promised." There was no way I could tell her. "Let's go get purple-and-green speckled glasses."

"Florence said there's a good place right over on Broadway." We walked for a bit. I tried to see if she really had stopped eating. Her face seemed about the same, but you couldn't tell much about her body inside the down jacket. "Thanks," she said. "For doing this for me."

"It's okay," I said.

"Are you mad at me? You seem sort of funny."

In spite of myself, out it popped: "Is David home?"

She looked at me. "Did you guys have a fight?"

"Did he say something?"

"No, just—he's been acting weird all week, and now you . . . Was it because of me?"

"Weird how?" I said.

"Touchy, foul-tempered. He's also started playing that depressing stuff on the guitar again, like with Michelle. And the only thing he said to me all week, practically, was 'Is Sarah still coming over?' "

My heart speeded up. "When was that?"

"Just now."

It speeded up some more. "What'd you tell him?"

"I told him yes, and we'd be back in a while."

"Did he say if he was going out?"

"David? He never tells anybody anything."

"I know." After all this time, I still had only a vague idea about his life.

Then we were at the glasses store. "I'll try not to take too long," she said as we went in. "We can take a cab back, if you want." She looked so sheepish and grateful and glad to be with me, I felt a surge of love for her.

But there were thousands of pairs to choose from, tens of thousands. And that's not counting the checkered ones and the pink plastic ones with earpieces coming from the bottom, like Mrs. Noonan's, the school lunchroom lady, and the ones that looked like something out of *Star Trek*.

"How do we do this?" she said, looking panicky.

"Got me." I sneaked a look at my watch: almost two.

If David was going to use those tickets, he'd have left by now.

"I just want something not too geeky."

A salesman walked toward us. "Need some help?" he said. Emily nodded. "Have a seat." He led us to a desk in front of the wall of glasses. Emily sat down and I stood behind her; he took down a few pairs, "Just to get a feel," he said.

She'd only tried the first two when her hands went to her mouth. "Oh no!" she cried. I turned to see what she was looking at. "I knew it! I just knew she'd do this to me."

And in walked Florence, in this black-and-white-spotted fake fur coat that didn't look like any animal I'd ever seen, except possibly a dalmatian. "I just happened to be passing by," she said, "and I saw you through the window, and I said to myself, let me just *step* in and say hello to Sarah! Sarah, you look *so* grown up, I hardly *recognized* you." Her voice, as usual, was so loud that everyone in the store turned to look at me. "So, have you two picked out anything yet?"

"We just got here." Emily's voice was like ice.

"Don't worry. I'm not going to interfere. This is entirely your choice." She turned to the salesman. "George, I hope she's not giving you too bad a time. She can be rather, how shall I say it, particular." She pulled up a chair. "George is a genius with frames. He's helped me for years."

I glanced at Florence's thick, goldfish-bowl glasses, then at Emily.

"No problem," said George. "I was just about to show her these Ralph Lauren frames. Sophisticated, yet dainty."

"Maybe, but they're so drab," Florence said. "I promise I'll stay out of it, but I'd rather she had something that adds a little color to her face. She gets so washed-out-looking at this time of year." I could see Emily's jaw tighten. "It's not an insult. We all do, sweetheart."

"Well, then, why don't we try these pink ones here," George said.

"*Icchh!*" Emily said, as soon as she put them on.

"A lot of the girls are choosing pink. But if you want to go a different route . . ." He handed her a red-framed pair.

She flopped back in her seat. "They all make my cheeks look like a chipmunk."

"They do not," Florence said.

"They do too. Look at them. I look like a rodent."

I'd seen a hundred of these battles, mostly about eating. Not only was it horribly embarrassing, it was using up a lot of time. I checked my watch again. Two-thirty-five. My mother was meeting the 5:09.

Emily noticed. Her eyes flicked to mine, then glanced away. She suddenly seemed embarrassed, too, which struck me as something new, something encouraging. Last summer, she'd been so caught up in the struggle, it was as if no one else existed.

I cleared my throat, then woofed under my breath.

"I know," Emily muttered, not looking at me. "I know."

Florence handed her another pair of glasses. They were perfectly reasonable glasses. Emily picked them up, but then put them down without trying them. "Florence?" she said.

"Is there a problem?" Florence said.

Emily looked at me. Say it, I mentally commanded her. Tell her.

Emily took a deep breath. "Do you think you could leave?"

"It's true, Ms. Friedman," George, the salesman, said, before Florence could say anything. "We're really doing fine here."

Florence's eyes got huge and googly behind her glasses. "Well," she said, wounded. "Fine. If that's what you want."

Emily's voice was stronger now. "I promised Sarah we would do this fast, because . . ." She hesitated and looked at me. "It's getting late and there's . . . this person she needs to see."

"Well," Florence said again. "The last thing I want is to hold anybody up. I'll just go home. Sarah, you're welcome to come back for dinner, after you finish your urgent business. And if you want to sleep over, we'd love to have you."

"Hi. Bye. Die," Emily said the instant she was out the door. George tried not to smile.

"That was pretty good," I said.

She took a deep breath and blew it out. "Yeah, well it works much better with you here. And I didn't say what I wanted to. You know, when she said, is there a problem?"

"Who cares," I said. "She left. Plus, I'm sure you'll have another chance." I looked at my watch again. "Can we please get this over with?"

"It's okay. We're not in a rush anymore," she said. "Not if you're sleeping over."

Chapter 11

"So . . ." David leaned against the doorway as if nothing were wrong. "Did you get the rhinestone-studded spectacles?" He'd walked past Emily's room almost as soon as we got back, then, a minute later, reappeared.

"Excuse you?" Emily said. "They're not spectacles." *Sassy* is not a word you'd normally use to describe Emily, but ever since she'd told Florence to leave, she'd been acting pretty bold. "They're eyewear, I'll have you know, from the Eyewear Emporium."

She launched into a detailed description, but I didn't hear a word. It seemed impossible that David felt as casual as he was acting. If he were that relaxed, he would have looked at me, unless he was either still angry or had suddenly turned shy. But he wasn't that shy, because he'd come into the room and was edging closer to the bed where Emily and I were sitting.

"You'll never guess who showed up," I said.

"Big Flo?" I could see it was an effort for him not to look at me.

"Yup!" Emily said.

"But Emily beat her back," I said. " 'Florence, would you mind just leaving?' That's what she said. And Florence left."

"She likes them, though," Emily said. "We showed them to her just now and she likes them."

"Oh, that's a relief." David's voice dripped sarcasm.

"Well . . ." Emily stood up. She looked at me and then at David. "I guess I'll go in the other room or something now."

"She's doing so great," I said, after she'd left. "I was worried about her when she called, but it seems as if things are okay."

"Yeah." He went over to Emily's desk and picked up a rubber band.

"So is she, like, eating like a normal person?"

He twisted the rubber band around his fingers till they were all hitched together. "I wouldn't go that far."

"That was pretty brave, what she did with Florence." If Emily could be brave, I could be, too. "So what happened with the tickets?"

"I gave them to a guy at school."

"What were they for?"

"Guitar concert. No big deal." He unwound the rubber band. "They were freebies. My teacher gets them all the time."

"So you're not still angry?" I was not brave enough to bring up the cello group.

"I wasn't angry," he said.

Right. There was a huge silence, until I said, "Florence invited me to sleep over tonight."

"Oh yeah?" He shot the rubber band across the room. "So are you?" It landed beside the bed. I leaned over and picked it up.

"I haven't asked my parents."

"Are you going to?"

"Should I?"

Suddenly all this tiptoeing around seemed so stupid, I shot the rubber band at him. It hit him in the ear. He looked so outraged, I burst out laughing.

"Oh, ha ha!" he said, which made me laugh some more.

"You look just like Florence when you're mad," I said. "Like this incredibly pissed-off pigeon."

"Die, scum!" he said, but I could tell then, from the way his eyes softened, that things would be all right.

So I did call my parents, who decided they'd drive in to the city the next morning and pick me up and we'd go out for brunch.

"That's wonderful!" Florence said. Except for the over-brightness of her smile, you wouldn't have known she'd just gone through a major humiliation. "It'll be just like old times, having you here again. Of course, now we're a quartet instead of just a trio." She glanced at my cello then, so I couldn't tell if she meant it or David.

Dinner, she declared, was going to be takeout Chinese. In the spirit of togetherness, she had us all sit down in the dining room with a stack of menus. David carefully did not look at me. "David likes hot peppers," she said, "but Emily always wants one of those soggy steamed things with no seasoning."

"Not always," Emily said. "I might want something different."

Florence didn't say anything. As a matter of fact, aside from pushing me to play something for them on the cello and commenting on the grease content of every dish, she stayed pretty quiet all through dinner. So did David, who'd taken the chair across from me but was actively pretending we didn't know each other. I was a mite tense myself, so I didn't say much, either.

We all sat there rolling our moo shu pork into our pancakes (or, in Emily's case, picking at the Hunan shrimp balls) till Florence said, "Oh, look! What fun. They sent us extra fortune cookies." She poured a pile of paper packets onto the table, then handed them around. "Sarah, you first."

" 'The path of life is strewn with many boulders,' " I read.

"Mine says I will journey to many lands," Emily said.

Florence opened hers. "Oho! 'Prepare for change.' I wonder what that means. David you next. This one looks promising." She handed him a cookie. He cracked it open, read the fortune, shifted in his seat, but didn't say anything.

"What is it?" Florence said. "Read it."

"Yeah, David, what does it say?" Emily said, giving me a look.

"Nothing. It's stupid," he said, crunching it up.

"It can't be that bad." Florence reached across and grabbed it. "What could it be? 'You will get your hair cut Monday?' Not that I mind your hair. I'm used to it. It's your father . . ." She unfolded the fortune and read out loud, " 'You will be lucky in love.' " And choked. But before she did, I could have sworn her eyes flicked right to me.

David left quickly after that, but Florence made microwave popcorn and insisted that Emily and I sit with her in the living room and watch a video. I don't even remember what it was. After a few minutes, I announced I was going to the bathroom.

"I'll pause it," Florence said.

"No, that's okay," I said. "I'll be right back."

I walked past the bathroom to David's room. He'd left his door open enough so I could see him lying on his bed. "You think she knows?" I said from the doorway.

"I couldn't tell for sure." He put his book down. "Did she say anything?"

I shook my head. "She's just acting all hearty and cheerful."

"That's never a good sign. Let's pray she doesn't know." He stood up, giving me this incredibly intense look.

We both stood there, sort of frozen, staring at each

other, until Florence started calling, "Sarah, you done in there? You're missing all the funny parts."

He groaned. "You better go," he said. I didn't want to. I really didn't want to, but as I turned to leave, he whispered, "Listen. Come back. After Emily's asleep. And don't say anything to her, either, just come. I'll be here waiting."

Chapter 12

I managed, somehow, to sit through the movie, though my heart was thumping so hard I was sure Florence could hear.

"So, do you think she knows?" I said when Emily and I were finally in bed, with the light off.

"Florence knows everything," Emily said. "It's, like, her life's work."

"Seriously, Emily." I wished I could see her face. "Does she know about me and David?"

"I don't think so. But she was looking at you a little funny. By the way, I meant to tell you, she's started therapy."

"I don't think it's started working yet," I said.

She giggled. "Yeah, that thing she said about David's hair, I thought he was going to throw a wonton at her." We lay there for a few minutes without talking. Then she said, "So, are things okay with you guys now?"

" 'Yeah," I said, not saying anything about going to his room. "Is everything okay with us? With you and me?"

"Yeah," she said.

"So we're still friends?"

"Yeah. We're still friends."

There was another long silence. Then I said, "So you can deal with this?"

"I guess so. If you can deal with David."

I wanted to ask what she meant, but I wanted even more for her to hurry up and go to sleep, so I didn't pursue it. I lay there till her breathing evened out, which seemed to take forever. Then I got up, put on the robe Florence had lent me, and tiptoed out into the hall. I could see light filtering under Florence's door and hear the faint sounds of her TV.

Slowly, carefully, I opened David's door. His room was dark except for his reading light. I went in.

He pulled off his headphones, jumped up from his bed, and closed the door. He still had his clothes on. I wished I had clothes on instead of Florence's ruffled robe and her long, fuzzy, baggy, peach-colored nightgown.

"What are you listening to?" I asked.

He didn't answer. He just pressed me against the wall till I could feel the whole length of his body and kissed me for a long time—serious kissing, till my knees were so limp I had to sit down on his bed.

"I couldn't stand that I wasn't going to see you today," he said. "That's why I was mad. It wasn't the tickets."

"I just needed to be with Emily," I said. "She's my friend. You understand that, right?"

He reached down and untied the sash of Florence's robe. Then he clasped his hands around my waist and I put my arms around him and we kissed again. He ran his hands all up my sides and kissed my neck.

I shivered, even though I wasn't cold. "I look like Florence in this outfit," I said.

"No," he said. "You do not look like Florence." He touched my hair. "You look like Sarah. My beautiful Sarah."

I don't know which got to me the most, the *my* or the *beautiful*, or the sort of husky catch in his voice, but my throat suddenly got all tight, and I felt weird, as if I was going to cry. Mostly it was happiness, but there was this strange sadness in there, too, that I didn't understand.

We lay back on the bed and I put my hands on his back inside his T-shirt and we kissed some more. "When I'm not with you, I miss you," he said, running his hands over my body. "You're trembling. You don't have to be scared. Nothing has to happen if you don't want it to." He said it so seriously it made me tremble harder. "I really love you, Sarah."

I didn't answer. I couldn't, so I kissed him. But when the kiss ended, he raised up on his elbow. "Do you love me?"

I did. It was different, though, writing it on a piece of paper, discussing it with Shelley, and being here with him and feeling it. Feeling it so strongly my bones felt as if they were going to dissolve. So I just nodded. He leaned into me and kissed me hard. "I'm scared, though," I said.

"Me too," he said.

"I never loved anyone before."

He moved back so he was leaning against the wall and I was lying with my head in his lap. From underneath, his eyelashes looked very long. "Me neither," he said. "Not like this."

"What about Michelle?"

"Michelle was different. With her it was, like, mainly sexual."

My heart began to pound, whether from excitement, fear, or jealousy, or just hearing the word out loud, I couldn't tell. "What was she like?" I asked, trying to sound as if it were a routine question.

"I don't know. She had really long blonde hair with these, like, tiny braids around her face. Like this." He combed his fingers through my hair, then separated off a strand and began braiding it. "She looked sort of medieval. She played the flute and she sang, but mostly she, like, languished."

"You make her sound so romantic. Like Rapunzel or somebody." Though what I was really thinking about was the sex part. "So what happened?"

He shrugged. "She wrote every day and then she stopped. I called her, because I thought she was coming here to see me, and she said she met somebody else. But it doesn't matter now, does it?" He put on a Transylvanian accent. "Because I have you, *mon petit chou*."

"What does that mean?" I said.

"It's French for 'my little cabbage.' "

"So why are you talking like Dracula?"

He laughed. "It must be your *loffly* neck. It drives me vild vit desire."

"You traded this medieval princess for a Brussels sprout?"

"Obsolutely! Moch more succulent, my little Brussels sprout!" By now we were both laughing. "Dahlink!" He leaned down and gave me a messy vampire kiss. "Will you be my Brussels sprout?"

I giggled at his gargled *r*s. "I just got over being an artichoke. Now you want me to be your Brussels sprout?"

Suddenly he froze. "Shhh!" he whispered, pulling away from me.

"What?" I was still laughing. "What is it?"

"My mother!"

Sure enough, I heard footsteps. I struggled to sit up and quickly wiped my mouth. There was a loud thump. He cursed. "She must not have put her glasses on." The footsteps stopped. "Did you close Emily's door?"

"Uh-oh," I whispered back.

He cursed again. "Let's hope she's too blind to notice you're not there."

We sat, not breathing, waiting for his door to be flung open.

But a minute later I heard her clump back to her room. "Whew!" I said. "What was she doing?"

"Either going to the kitchen or on patrol. Or both."

"Does she know I'm in here?"

"Nah." He shook his head. "Or she'd have burst in here like a charging rhino." He put his arm around me. But before we could relax again, we heard the footsteps coming back.

David groaned. "Forget it! She's eating." He lay back with his hands behind his head and closed his eyes. "Once she gets started . . . I should have known. I should have known we couldn't be together here. I knew I should have moved in with my dad."

"Shhh," I said, leaning over him to put my finger to his lips, thinking I'd do anything to get the tender, romantic, silly David back. "It doesn't matter. She didn't come in, right? And we are together. It's okay."

"No, it's not," he said. "She's going to be marching back and forth till there's nothing left in the whole kitchen but the soy sauce and the tea bags. The first trip was probably the drink. Now you can bet she's going back to finish off the fortune cookies. The third trip, she'll get into the moo shu pork and anything else that isn't nailed down." He sat up and straightened his shirt. "Which will give you at least thirty seconds to get back to Emily's room. I'll tell you one thing, though. Next week, I'm going to find someplace where we can be alone."

He looked so furious and sad and disappointed, I couldn't possibly tell him I had the cello group the next Saturday.

Chapter 13

"Great news!" David's voice on the telephone sounded all excited. It was Wednesday night, around eleven. "I have a place for us for Saturday!"

My stomach plummeted. I still hadn't gotten the nerve to tell him about the cello group. We'd talked every day, but our talks had been so full of all the missing each other stuff, I dreaded saying anything to spoil it.

"My dad has a girlfriend. I just had dinner with him. It's a person in his office—Kelly, Tracy, some name like that."

"Does Florence know?" I asked. What Florence knew and didn't know was still very much on my mind, though it was clear she still hadn't caught on about me and David.

"I have no idea. That's not the point. The point is, he told me tonight the two of them are going out to Montauk for the weekend. He was like, 'Son, I hope you can understand.' " David made his voice sound pompous. " 'She's a lovely young woman, full of vitality and warmth, and I have to live my life. I know you must have feelings about this.' And I'm like, 'No, Dad, honestly, it's fine,' thinking, Yes! Great! Go! Goodbye! Because now we can use his place Saturday. He's leaving Friday night, right after work, and he won't be back till Sunday—"

"David," I said. His timing was particularly unfortunate. I'd just spent the whole night practicing. The Goltermann was going really well, and "Song of the Birds" was just starting to sound good. "I have a small problem about Saturday." I took a deep breath. "Miss Hauptman asked me to join her cello group. It's, like, this really big honor. It means she thinks I'm good enough. Which is not bad, right, considering I've only been studying with her since January. And it wasn't like she *asked* me. She practically commanded me."

"I get the point," David said. "You want to do it. Fine."

"I sort of have to. But I also want to. You'd want to, too, wouldn't you?"

"I'd want to be with you," he said.

I felt this terrible pull—worse, even, than with Emily. "Even if your teacher gave you a chance like this?"

"I'm sure this group meets all the time. Who knows when you and I will get another chance like this. You've met Elliott. Think about it. How likely is it this Tracy/ Stacy person will want to be with him again?"

"I know," I said. "I'm sorry." I could picture his face,

his mouth all tight, but his eyes sweet and full of hurt. "What about if we see each other from one to two-thirty? We could go to the park . . ."

"Oh, thanks a lot," he said. "Thanks for your generosity. I get to have a big fat hour and a half of your time."

This was sounding horribly like our last fight. "David, please," I said, "I do want to be with you. Really. Can you try to understand my side of it?"

"You sound like my father. He finally has dinner with me and all he wants to talk about is his warm and vital twenty-two-year-old girlfriend. Why am I always the one who has to understand, who has to fit into everybody else's life? I love you, Sarah. I want to be with you. I want to be somewhere with you where we can be by ourselves. Alone."

I'd been lying on my bed, but now I took the phone and walked over to the window. I could see the neighbor's dog in the yard across the street, sniffing at a garbage can. "Miss Hauptman and I played this duet last week, this really beautiful Handel sonata for two cellos. I played it really well. You should have heard us, David. I couldn't believe how beautiful we sounded. I couldn't have done that without you. You made it possible. You made it happen."

"What does that mean?"

I couldn't bear the stiffness in his voice. "It's because of how I feel about you. It's, like, permeated my whole life. It's opened up everything. It's changed how I can play."

"How wonderful for you."

"David, please," I said. "Don't be sarcastic. I do want to do the cello group, but I'm trying to tell you something. You and music. That's all I care about. And they're, like, totally tied up together. One doesn't work without the other. Do you understand what I'm saying?"

"Not really." He still sounded grudging.

We had variations on that exact same conversation every night that week, but he did, eventually, seem to understand, because Saturday, when I came out of my lesson, there he was, waiting for me in the fifth-floor lounge.

I rushed over and threw my arms around him. "I'm performing the Bach *Arioso*," I said. I liked the way that sounded: *I'm performing*. "My lesson went really well."

He handed me a bag. "I brought you something."

"What is it?" I practically ripped open the container.

"Noodle soup," he said. "From that Japanese restaurant you liked." He had this shy, expectant look. "I know it's a strange present, but it's really good. It's got shrimp and meat and stuff in it. I started to get sushi, but then I thought cold raw fish might seem a little weird . . ."

"No, this is great," I said. "It's perfect. How did you know I was dying for something Japanese?" I hadn't known myself until that instant.

"I know you, remember?" He put his arm around me. "You told me I'm your muse, right? Your inspiration. I take the job seriously. I even got this special Japanese hot mustard to put on it, in case you're nervous. It's exactly like wasabi."

"I love wasabi," I said.

"Why do you think I got it? Plus, wasabi's guaranteed to blast any nervousness right out of you." He looked me over. "Though you don't really look that nervous."

I snuggled in against him, which is not easy with lunch in one hand and a cello hanging from your other shoulder. "I'm too happy to be nervous."

I was actually as much hyper as happy. We ended up eating our soup on a bench in the center island of Broadway because Central Park felt too far away from the conservatory. It wasn't exactly romantic, slurping up noodles from a plastic container with people tromping past and taxis, trucks, and buses roaring by, but he'd brought a lot of napkins. It was one of those bright March days when even New York City air smells good and you can't stand to keep your jacket on another second, and somehow all that made the spicy soup seem even more delicious.

"Isn't your knee cold?" I said, fingering the big rip in his jeans.

He pressed my hand down on his leg. "Yeah, warm it up for me." We set the containers on the bench and ate one-handed—he with his arm around me to keep me warm, I with my hand cupped over his knee—feeling the hot glow of the spicy mustard in our throats, our hair blowing in our faces. It was somewhat messy, and I had to keep taking my hand away to check my watch.

"Relax," he said. "We've got plenty of time. Plus, you told me that she said this isn't a recital. Didn't she say it's just a chance to try out your musical ideas in front of people and iron out the wrinkles in your performance?"

"Yes, I know. . . ." I'd quoted that to him at least six times.

"So stay here." He nuzzled my neck and gave me his Count Dracula leer. "I'll iron out your wrinkles, my little Brussels sprout."

I giggled. "David, I can't. I just want to make sure I'm ready."

"You'll be ready," he said, slipping his hand up inside my shirt. "You've been practicing all week."

"*Youch!*" I shrieked, as his fingers touched my back. "Your hand feels like ice." But his mouth was warm and we did stay a while longer, kissing spicy-mustard kisses, till I got too fidgety and said we had to leave.

"You better pray for me this goes all right," I said, as we walked up the street to the conservatory. I stopped outside the door but didn't let go of David's hand. "I've never done this before. What if I bomb? What if my fingers are so cold I can't play?"

"You won't bomb," he said. "You're going to be great."

"I hope so. Wish me luck."

"You don't need luck," he said, giving me one last kiss. "You've got me. And cellist's eyebrows. And wasabi power!"

Chapter 14

"What are you playing?" An Asian woman in a dress and pearls fell into step beside me as I walked down the hall.

"What are you playing?" asked a second dressed-up Asian woman sitting on a bench outside the room as I went in.

"So, what are you playing today?" The room buzzed with the same question. People glanced up briefly as I came in, but then immediately went back to tuning and comparing pieces: " 'Lalo.' " "Oh, I hate the Lalo." " 'Haydn C Major.' I'm doing it with the Paramus Symphony in April." "Schumann. You know, I'm performing it next Saturday." In the front row, a short Asian kid hunched over his cello practicing, while in the back, two earnest girls whispered as they rubbed rosin on their bows.

For all my endless fantasizing about this afternoon, the only part I'd focused on was me. I'd barely thought about the other people. There were eight of them, I saw now, most about my age, all acting and talking as if they'd done this every day since they were born. I recognized nobody except Natalie, who'd given me a tight, snooty smile when I came in. Miss Hauptman had smiled, too, but now she had her hand on the shoulder of a tall, skinny boy in a baseball cap and was too busy lecturing him to pay attention to me.

I brought my cello to the back of the room, which was bigger than the one in which I had my lesson, with rows of folding chairs and a grand piano and school auditorium-like draperies at the windows. I unpacked; checked my tuning; rosined my bow, which didn't need rosining; then took a seat in the last row, sitting on my hands to try to get them warm. The name-dropping continued: "Popper Spinning Wheel." "Oh, *bummer*." "First movement of the 'Brahms E Minor.'" "You're *still* working on the Brahms?" That was Natalie. "I thought you knew, I'm preparing it for the Shnoobitsky Competition."

"Try to ignore them." A girl in the row ahead of me turned and gave me a wry smile. "They're always like this before these things." I thought of David and his wasabi power and tried to smile back, but I have no idea what it came out like.

Suddenly the chatter stopped. A man in a suit walked through the door, the two Asian women close behind him. The man nodded to Miss Hauptman and arranged himself at the piano. Everyone scrambled to find a seat. The tension level in the room went up about fifty notches. Miss Hauptman looked right at me. "We've got someone new joining us today," she said, introducing me.

"You're on!" the girl in front of me whispered. "So what are you playing?"

My head began to fill with booming noises, as if someone had clamped two giant seashells on my ears. But Miss Hauptman called "Lynn," and a tiny, long-haired girl in a party dress and ruffled socks went up, handed the pianist her music, and tore into the first movement of the "Saint-Saëns Concerto."

What was I doing here? I could practice twenty-four hours a day and I still couldn't play that fast. Or that intensely. Or get a giant sound like that out of her dinky, half-sized cello.

When Lynn finished, Miss Hauptman showered her with praise, then made some suggestions, which the lady in the pearls, who must have been her mother, wrote down on a pad. Don't make me follow her, I prayed. But Miss Hauptman called the kid in the baseball cap. I don't remember what he played, but he had a gorgeous sound and long, elegant fingers and a terrific bow arm, and, once again, Miss Hauptman was full of praise.

She was full of praise for everybody, which was not surprising. They were all great: the tall, handsome guy named Seung, who played Beethoven; then the short kid, whose mother, the other lady, also took extensive notes; then one of the earnest girls, playing something ridiculously technical.

And Miss Hauptman was amazing. Maybe I was just too overawed to hear the flaws, but I'd be sitting there thinking these guys couldn't possibly play any better, and she'd make some tiny comment, or sing a phrase, or walk over and adjust their hand position, zooming in on some problem I didn't even know existed, and they'd play it again and it would be incredibly improved.

If I were a more wonderful human being, that would have made me happy. But right then, it made me even more jealous and despairing.

When at last it was my turn, my hands, which had never warmed up completely, turned colder than sushi and my throat got so tight I was sure I couldn't swallow.

But, weird as it sounds, part of me still clung to the idea that I was good. Okay, Sarah, don't slump, I told myself as I went to the back and got my cello. Don't sniff or snort or screw your mouth up or hold your breath. I walked up the aisle, handed my music to the pianist, and sat down. Don't overtighten your bow. Try not to look as if you're going to barf.

So how was I? At first, I was just relieved there were no disasters: I didn't break a string; my end pin didn't suddenly loosen, sending my cello on a slow slide to the floor; Miss Hauptman didn't stop me for anything humiliating. But by the time I reached the first repeat, I started liking being up there in front of everybody. I loved Bach. I liked the *Aricso*, even if it was sort of a corny piece. And the pianist was such a pro, he could make anyone sound good. But it wasn't just that. I'd gotten better. Listening to the other players, or absorbing Miss Hauptman's advice to them, or maybe performing for an audience had made me play better than I'd played in my entire life. I sounded like a cellist.

So I was astounded when they didn't clap for me. The pianist gave me a warm smile, and I could see from Miss Hauptman's eyes that she was pleased, but the other kids were either giggling and tittering among themselves or looking as if they could hardly stay awake. I felt them staring as I walked back down the aisle, but nobody said "Wow, that was great" or "nice job" or anything.

One more girl played after me, but I heard nothing. And at the end, when everyone rushed up to talk to Miss Hauptman, and the name-dropping and note-comparing began again, I grabbed my cello and headed for the door. I couldn't stand the thought of meeting any of them at the elevator, so I took the stairs.

I felt so humiliated, it didn't dawn on me to be surprised to see David waiting in the lobby.

"Let's get out of here," I said, before he could say hi or anything. "What was I thinking?" I started to walk with no idea where I was going, walking so fast the cello knocked against my side. "What was I even doing there? They all played concert pieces, Yo Yo Ma–type pieces, Rostropovich pieces."

"Yeah, but how did yours go?"

"Let's just say it was like I was on Book One while the rest of them were at Book Two Thousand and Forty-Five."

"So what?" he said.

"So you should have seen the way they looked at me, like I was a total lamer, like I was some old limp bologna sandwich and they were, I don't know, caviar soufflé."

"Screw 'em!" he said. "How'd *you* think you were?"

"Talk about delusions of grandeur . . . I thought I was good. That's what makes it even more pathetic."

"What do you care what they think? You don't want to be like them. You don't want anything to do with them."

"I know." I sighed. Even though a big part of me was crying, yes, I do! I want to be just like them. I want to be better than them.

"I hate all that pretentious, stuck-up crap! I can just hear them, going on about where they're auditioning and their recitals and their prizes, basking in their wonderfulness."

"How d'you know?"

"Juilliard, remember? Plus the music camp I worked at. Not to mention my school's crawling with idiots like that. Have you stopped to consider that maybe they were jealous of you?"

"Of me?" I said. "Miss Lamer? Miss Beginner? Right."

"Hey, it's possible."

"You only say that because you haven't heard me," I said, even though my heart had started beating faster. "And don't even bother woofing."

He stopped walking. "So play for me."

"Now?" I felt a sudden stab of terror and excitement. "You want to hear me play? What, the stupid *Arioso*?"

"Yeah. Or 'Song of the Birds.' Whatever. Why not?"

By this time we were almost all the way to Broadway. "I'm not going back there," I said, shaking my head. "They're probably all still up there. I can't deal with seeing them."

"You don't have to," David said, taking my arm. "We'll go over to my dad's."

Chapter 15

"So do you want something to eat or drink or anything?" David asked.

"No thanks," I said. I'd talked the whole way over in the cab but now, standing in Elliott Friedman's living room, neither one of us could think of anything to say.

"Aren't you going to take your jacket off?" he said.

"Oh. Right." It felt as if there were some weird, electric force field around each of us. The room thrummed with it. I could hear it in our voices, feel the tingle of it in my palms.

I set my cello down and pulled off my jacket. "Should I, like, hang it up?" I said, looking around the luxurious, all-white living room. "Everything here's so neat. I don't want to mess anything up."

"We're all alone," David said. "We can do anything we want."

"Well . . . ," I said, after I'd draped my jacket on a

chair, "I guess I'd better play." I pulled a straight chair over to the middle of the room, unpacked my cello, sat down, adjusted my end pin, and checked my tuning. "This has to be the cleanest apartment in the world," I said. "It's like the Waldorf Astoria or something. It's the complete opposite of your mom's house. No offense."

He sat down on the white sofa facing me and put his feet on the gleaming glass coffee table. "Yeah, well, I guess that's what he wanted, a completely new life."

I tightened my bow. "How long has he lived here?"

"He moved out Christmas Eve a year ago. Merry Christmas, right?"

"But you see him every week," I said.

"Yeah, for a few hours. When he says so." He stopped. "Sarah," he said, looking at me so hard I could barely breathe.

I put my bow down and wiped my hands on my pants. "Okay. Stop stalling, Sarah. Here goes." For two months now I'd dreamed of David hearing me play. But I never imagined we'd be here, like this, alone. "I'm playing now," I said. "You ready for this?" Without meeting his eyes again, I picked up my bow and played the *Arioso*. It felt to me as if I played it even better than at the workshop.

"Nice," he said when I was done.

"For real?" I still didn't dare look at him.

"Yeah." He nodded slowly, seriously. "You have a great sound. Is that, like, a really good cello or is that you?" I told him we'd bought it from an ad in the paper.

"So it is you."

My chest swelled with pleasure. Or maybe it was just relief at breathing again.

"And it wasn't corny. It was full of feeling. I knew it." His eyes were glowing. "I knew you'd be really good."

"Sure. Because I was playing something simple and beginnerlike." More. More compliments, keep talking, I felt like saying.

"That's such a load of crap!" David sat up. "Those people are such jerks. If the cello's anything like the guitar, even the simple things are really hard if you're trying to do them really well. That's what my teacher says. And you clearly are."

"I am," I said, feeling a flood of love and happiness and gratitude.

"I know you are. I was being serious. Want to know something, though? I'm glad they're jerks. We've got one less thing to ruin our Saturdays. Play something else for me. Play 'Song of the Birds.'"

My heart was pounding, but this time, as I played, I kept my eyes on him. I thought it might make me mess up, but it did the opposite.

"I am so happy I introduced this piece to you," he said when I was done. "You're so beautiful when you play." He came over, pushed back my hair, and kissed me on the neck. I could feel my blood whirring in my veins. "There's so much music in you, Sarah," he whispered. "It's really sensual. It's like all your passions are right there on your face for me to touch." He took off his glasses.

"Oh no!" I said. I'd suddenly remembered. "I didn't call my parents. I said this morning if I didn't call, they should be at the train station at six-twenty-five." I checked my watch. It was 6:17 now. I stood up and set my cello on the floor. "Where's the phone? I bet my dad already left." David went over to the desk and picked up a white cordless phone. "I can just hear him when he gets back and tells my mom I didn't show. What'll I say?" I said, as he handed it to me. "I can't tell them we're alone at Elliott's."

"Tell them you were abducted by aliens. Little green guys." He put his arms around me. "Say it was a command performance. They beamed you up briefly to play Bach."

"David, I'm being serious," I said. Though it was hard to be too serious with him kissing me.

"Then tell them you're at the Friedmans.' " Little kiss. "Say they invited you over." Another little kiss. "Say they missed you and really needed to be with you. Say they would have been miserable and lonely and upset if you didn't come." Big kiss. "It's true, Sarah. That's not a lie. I really do need to be with you."

But what I told my mother, after telling her I bombed, which I knew would make her feel sorrier for me, was that I was the one who was upset. "I was so upset I totally forgot to call," I said. Which was not a lie. "I really needed someone to talk about it with." I tried to sound as if I were still suffering. "And David's a musician. He knows about these things." I knew I shouldn't mention David. But he was behind me with his arms wrapped around my waist and when I said, "He's really good to talk to about stuff like this," he whispered, "Yeah. He's really good."

"You were supposed to come right home," my mother said. "Remember? You've got that bio project due Monday and you left it till the last minute."

I started to say I'd left it because I was so busy practicing, but I didn't dare piss her off further. Plus, David's hands were inching up inside my shirt, which made it really hard to concentrate. I leaned against him as she went to get the timetable. He kissed my neck, which sent shivers up and down my back, but I made my voice sound reliable and sincere as I promised to have someone walk me to a cab and to leave plenty of time to get to Penn Station, and to not, whatever I did, miss the 7:50 train.

"See how easy that was," David said, laughing, when I got off the phone. We were both laughing. "Piece of cake. We've got over an hour." We started kissing for real then, first leaning against the wall, then on the couch—incredibly sweet, soft kisses, then harder, more intense ones. "This is my bed, you know," he murmured, his hands sliding up inside my clothes. "It opens up. When I stay over here, this is where I sleep."

My brain felt like it had turned to gauze, my legs all

weak and floaty. I could easily have stayed like that forever, feeling him whisper in my hair, "Sarah, I love you.
You're so wonderful. I love you more than anything."

But then he unbuttoned my pants. "What are you
doing?" I said. My voice sounded furry and far away.

"Nothing," he whispered, pulling down the zipper.

"David, don't," I said, feeling a small tug of fear.

"Shhh." He put a finger on my lips. "It's okay. It's
nothing to be scared of." His voice was sweet, persuasive,
urgent. "It's just like music. You'll see. Like 'Song of the
Birds,' when you played it for me. Like the greatest music
you ever heard, only better. Please, Sarah."

"No," I said, louder, shaking my head. "Stop, David.
I can't do this."

"It's okay," he said again. "I promise. I've got protec-
tion."

Instantly I snapped from mental meltdown to full alert.
I'd both known and not known this might happen, but it
was one thing thinking about it by myself, in my own
room, where I never imagined details, just this romantic
sort of blur, and another being here and having to decide.
Or not decide, just sliding into it.

I sat up, pulled my zipper back up, and fumbled with
the button. "I can't," I said, straightening my shirt.

"Please," he begged, sitting up too, pulling me to him,
kissing my throat. "I want you so much, Sarah. Don't
you want me?" I didn't know whether to say yes or no. "I
thought you loved me."

"I do."

"This is how people show each other that they love each other." He smoothed my hair. "You said all you cared about was me and music. You said I'd opened you up. That I was what made music possible for you. Think how much better you'll play after you've opened up even more, after you've really made love . . ."

It was so hard to think with so many feelings swirling around, with his eyes burning into me, with him touching me. I edged back into the corner of the couch and folded my arms and tucked my legs under me. "This is scaring me, David. It's too fast. It doesn't feel right to me."

"Why not?"

I didn't dare look at him. "Because it doesn't."

"You're saying you don't care enough."

"I do care enough." I could hear my voice rising. "That's not the reason."

"I see. It's fine for me to, like, inspire you and be there for you and comfort you when you need something and are all upset, but when I ask you to give me something—"

"Wait." I was thinking straighter now. "I thought you just said it was for me. To make me a better musician."

"What's your reason?" he persisted. "You have to have a reason. People always have reasons for things."

"Stop pushing me," I said. "I don't have to know why not. I just have to know I don't want to be pushed into it. Maybe I'm not ready. This is all new to me, remember? Before I met you, I never even had a real boyfriend. Before I met you, my most intimate relationship was with a rhododendron bush." I was starting to get really angry, but looking at his face, all dark and closed, suddenly I felt scared, too, as if something beautiful and precious had slipped away from me. Which made me want to cry. I reached over and put my arms around him. His body felt rigid.

He pulled away from me and put his glasses back on, then went over to the kitchen area at the far end of the room and opened the fridge. "There's nothing to eat in this refrigerator," he said. His voice was harsh, but the set of his back—so stiff and obstinate, yet in some weird way defenseless—suddenly reminded me of Emily. I loved him enormously.

"David?" I said. He was looking in the freezer. "Even if I'm not ready now, I do love you." It was the first time I'd come right out and said the words. My ears began to boom again. My throat tightened. "You know that, right?"

He didn't turn around. "You've got a funny way of showing it. Not showing it. There's Cappuccino Commotion in here, but it's hard as a rock. You want some anyway?" He brought the container over with two spoons and sat down next to me. We tried to chisel some out, but it was frozen solid. "I could just nuke it in the microwave," he said. "Should I just try that?"

"David?" I said, as he managed to pry out a chocolate chunk. "I can't just do it because you want me to. If I do it, it's because it's my own decision and I'm totally ready . . ."

"Well, when will that be?" He shaved off a curl of ice cream and held it out to me.

I shook my head. "Don't do this to me, David," I said.

"You're the one doing it. Not doing it."

"Can we stop saying 'doing it'? I hate that term, 'doing it.'"

"All I'm asking is how long it's going to take you to work it out."

"I don't know."

"A week, a month, a year?" He gave me his Count Dracula leer, than grabbed me and kissed me. "Five minutes? We can take a cab."

"Would you give it a rest! You're so obnoxious sometimes," I said. Relieved to see him lighten up, I hit him with my spoon.

"How about the stupid ice cream, then?" he said. "Has that at least softened up?" He squeezed the container. "You may have rejected me—"

"I have not rejected you." I hit him again.

"But I will not be defeated by a pint of Häagen-Dazs." He began to jab the ice cream with his spoon.

I was almost sure we were joking around now, but something made me say, "Are you, like, really angry still?"

"I wasn't angry." He stopped poking at the ice cream and looked at me. His eyes were serious. "I just really need you is all. You're not still mad at me?"

I shook my head. "I wasn't mad, either," I said.

Chapter 16

So then things seemed to be okay again, if you don't count that I managed to miss the 7:50 train, pissing my parents off so completely that they said I had to come straight home after my lesson for the next three weeks. Which then got David all upset. But he didn't seem angry at me anymore. "I just want things to be all right with us," he told me on the phone. "I don't want to mess things up. If you need time, you can have it. You can have all the time you need."

I was relieved, but still totally unsettled. Except for practicing and talking to David, all I did that week was wait for Saturday.

The practicing paid off, though. "My goodness, Sarah," Miss Hauptman said at my next lesson. She'd changed the black suit for a bright green one and a silver pea-pod pin with three jade peas in it. "In honor of spring," she said. "You had another leap forward this week, didn't you? You're moving ahead fast. Yes," she went on, more to herself than me. "I really do have to get you playing with other people. There's the orchestra, of course, for next year, but I'd like to get you started sooner. A quartet would be perfect if we can find people the right level—good enough to be a challenge—"

"Miss Hauptman?" I couldn't keep my mouth shut. "Can I ask you something?" It was the same question I'd asked David the day we went for sushi, the same one I'd put to Emily when I first started. "I keep thinking about how good you have to be before you can call yourself a *cellist*."

She put down her bow and looked at me. The crease between her eyebrows deepened. "I'm not sure exactly what it is you're asking, Sarah."

I pulled a loose hair off my bow and twisted it around my finger. "I just keep thinking about all your other students and how good they are . . . "

"Are you asking me if you can be that good?"

My ears immediately filled up with the booming noises. "It's not just so I can be better than everybody. I don't mean that. That's not it."

"Aha. Better." Miss Hauptman's eyes were sparkling now. "You've got your work cut out for you, my dear."

"That's not what I meant to say," I said. I could have used a glass of water. "Really. I didn't mean it that way. That sounds so terrible."

"So what?" she said. "There's room in the world for

another cellist. Your being good doesn't make the others any less good."

I couldn't tell if I was going to explode from pride or burst from nervous pressure, so I said that thing I'd said to David once: "I wish there were a valve that I could open and it would make the music come out the way I hear it in my head."

"Don't we all," she said. "But it's the fact that you do hear it so clearly in your head that tells me you *can* be a cellist. Provided you keep working. Besides, if you had that valve, then you wouldn't need me, would you? Enough talk. Back to work."

Afterward, David was waiting for me outside the room. I threw myself into his arms. "I'm talented!" I said. "She says I'm talented."

"I could have told you that," he said. "I did tell you that last week. Don't I get a hello?"

"Hello!" I said, handing him my cello so I could put my jacket on. He looked particularly cool in his light-blue denim shirt and his leather jacket and his hair all fluffed out the way it got when he'd just washed it. "She thinks I can be a cellist! She wants to find a group for me. She says I need to play with other people."

"You can play with me," he said, hooking his arm around my neck as we walked to the elevator. I punched him. "I meant cello and guitar," he said. "I was being serious."

Just then, Seung, the tall, good-looking guy from the

cello group, appeared. "Hey," he said, smiling at me. "Sarah."

I couldn't believe he knew my name. "I really liked the way you played the Beethoven," I said, smiling too.

David's hand tightened on my back.

"Thanks," Seung said, friendly, peerlike. "You'll be there next time?"

"Yeah," I said, as he headed for the stairs.

We were still waiting for the elevator when I saw Miss Hauptman walking toward the ladies' room. "Miss Hauptman!" I called. "This is David. My friend. He's a musician."

"Ah," she said, coming over, smiling. "The guitarist. Too bad you're not a viola player. We always need good violists. Where are you two off to on this lovely afternoon?"

"Nowhere, unfortunately," I said. "I have to go straight home. I missed my train last week."

"Do you study here?" she asked David.

"No," he said.

"But he's terrific," I said. It was amazing how nervous I felt, having the two of them meet each other.

"Well, I'd love to hear you play sometime," she said, as the elevator doors opened and we got in.

"She's great, isn't she?" I said as we rode down.

"I just want to get out of here," David said.

"Oh, David," I said, taking his hand as we went out the door. "I don't want to go home." The air was warm.

Pink buds were swelling on the trees. "It's way too nice to get on the subway now."

"Then let's not," he said.

"But we have to get to that stupid train. If we don't, I'm dead."

"So we'll take a cab." He stepped into the street and put up his arm and, within seconds, a taxi stopped. He got in and I handed him the cello, then sat down next to him. "Alone at last!" he said, as soon as I closed the door. "It's about time!" And before the driver had gotten to the first light, we were kissing. Which was not totally comfortable while hurtling down Broadway with a cello lying across both our laps, but I felt way too good to mind.

"I feel so happy," I said when we finally came up for air.

"Me too," David said into my ear. His glasses were all steamed up and his voice was husky. "I've missed holding you. This week felt like forever."

"I know," I said, pressing closer against him. My voice sounded strange, too, and it was hard to breathe.

"I don't want to leave you," he said. "I wish we could just drive and drive."

Suddenly he sat up and cleared his throat and reached into his pocket. "Excuse me, sir," he said in a completely different tone. The taxi driver looked at us in his rearview mirror. "How much would it cost to drive us to Long Island?"

"What?" I said. "David, are you serious?"

He shrugged.

The driver frowned and shook his head. "Too much." He had heavy black eyebrows and a strong accent. "Very long trip. Bad traffic. Lot of money."

"How much is a lot?" David said.

We stopped for a red light and the driver turned around. "Where you going on Long Island?"

"You're seriously going to drive me home in a taxi-cab?" I said to David.

His eyes were sparkling. "It's a great idea, right? It gives us a whole extra hour." He raised the cello and caressed my leg, then gave it a squeeze. I told the driver where I lived.

"Eighty dollars," he said.

David quickly counted the money in his wallet. "How 'bout forty? Off the meter. You get to keep it all."

"Fifty," the driver said. "And you buy the gas."

"How much is that going to be?" I whispered. "Do you have that much?"

David had been doing a great imitation of a hard-nosed businessman, but now he rolled his eyes. "Yeah, if I don't eat lunch for the next month. . . ." He leaned toward the driver. "Let's do it. Long Gyland, here we come!"

With a screech of his brakes, the driver made a quick left turn, slamming me against David and David into the door. We grabbed on to each other, giggling, and David tried to kiss me again, but it was pretty hard to concentrate with the driver weaving through traffic, honking his horn, almost scraping the side of a delivery truck. He had also begun eating something that smelled like a meatball hero.

"Hey, man," David called, still laughing, "slow down. We're not in that big of a rush. Sarah and I want more time together, not less."

"Well, one thing," I said, "we're going to get home faster than the train." I clutched his arm as the cab bounced into a pothole and then had a near miss with a crosstown bus. "My parents can't be mad at me this time. And wait till Shelley sees me pull up to the house in a New York City taxi," I said as we went through the tunnel. "She is going to be so jealous. She's going to think we're really cool."

"We are really cool," David said.

"Also rich," I said. "What are you doing with all that money in your wallet?"

"I was going to buy guitar strings after you left."

"Is that a guitar?" the driver asked. He'd finished his sandwich and had moved on to a banana. Ever since David had pulled out money for the tunnel and paid for gas and we'd helped the driver figure out on a map where we were going, we'd become his new best friends.

"No," I said, "a cello." You get that question at least once a day when you carry around a cello, but at the moment, even that struck me as funny. "David plays guitar."

"This is very nice," the driver said, giving us benevolent looks in his mirror. "I like this. Two music lovers who are also lovers. I love music. I had a musician in my cab last week, a violinist—"

"Cool," David said. "I'm happy for you." He put his other arm around me and pulled me close.

But just as we started to get into it, the driver asked, "So, you go to the university?"

"No." David was clearly trying to end the conversation.

"I went to university in my country."

I couldn't help myself. I had to ask, even though David was giving me shut-up-Sarah looks. "What country is that?"

"Afghanistan."

"You're kidding," I said.

David poked me.

"I went to medical school. You think I'm a just a taxi driver, but in my country, I'm a doctor. A gynecologist."

That shut me up. And after a minute David moved his mouth toward mine and the driver didn't interrupt until we reached my exit and he needed me to give directions to my street. And when we reached my house, I said what David had said a little while before: "I wish we could drive forever."

"I'm going to really miss you," I said as we slowly walked, arms around each other, to my door.

"Good," he said. "Miss me a lot. Think about me all week."

"Don't worry," I said.

"I'm going to talk to my dad," he whispered in my ear. "See if he can find something to do next Saturday and leave me the apartment." He ran his hand up and down my side. "I'm thinking you're not going to need that much more time."

Chapter 17

"How far are you from the ocean?" he asked me on the phone that night. "I want to go to the ocean with you."

"That'd be so great," I said. "It's not that far."

"If I had a car, we could drive there," he said. "We could drive anywhere, go anywhere we want, do anything. We could really be alone."

"I didn't know you could drive," I said.

"My dad'll teach me," he said. "I've got some money saved, and if I earn some more and my parents give me cash for my birthday, I can probably get some kind of car by the summer. We'll go to the beach every day, hang out, stay till it's dark. Think about it, Sarah—you and me, the moon, the stars, the pounding surf. I can't wait till summer."

* * *

"I keep thinking about us on that beach," he told me the next night. "You and me on a blanket, all alone. Are you thinking about it, too?"

How could I not be?

"Are you thinking about . . . you know . . . us?" Whispering, in case I didn't know exactly what he meant.

"You said there was no rush," I said.

"I know," he said. "I just want you to be thinking about it. 'Cause I'm thinking about it. A lot."

It was pretty much all I thought about. It was like when I was about to get a bra and suddenly became acutely conscious that the entire world was wearing bras. But it wasn't all the naked Calvin Klein ads that got to me, or the sitcoms, or the kids pawing each other in the stairwell and all over each other in the parking lot. It was seeing Fishface, my stand partner in orchestra—Rachel Karp, whom I'd been so sure was more socially backward than I was. There we are, sawing away at "Eine Kleine Nacht-musik," and I suddenly notice that Kevin Banzoff from the second violin section isn't playing because he's doing something with his bow inside her pant leg. And Timmy Dolan, who still looked exactly like he did in kindergarten, with his hands all over Ariana Klingman. And Lindsay Lockwood, who wore her Girl Scout uniform to school till the seventh grade, in a major clinch with the guy from Pizza Hut. The list goes on and on: Mr. Strolich, the algebra teacher, whom I spotted coming out of the teacher's lounge with Ms. Caputo, both of them with extremely unteacherly smirks on their faces. The neighbors' dogs. My parents. (Okay, maybe that one's a bit of a stretch.) Shelley and Bart.

"It's not that big a thing," Shelley said, when I very tentatively brought it up. This will give you some clue about my state of mind, that I even considered discussing my future sex life with my sister. "And you *have* been seeing him every week for three months." She made herself comfortable on my bed. "And you do love him, right? And I can take you to my doctor." I had a sudden, hideous vision of the taxi driver and his meatball hero. "If you promise not to say anything to Mom."

I would have liked to have had the kind of mom I could say something to. But with my parents, things work best when you don't say anything. They've made not saying anything into a way of life.

"So are you going to do it?" Shelley asked.

"You sound just like David," I said.

"I've worked it out," he announced the next Saturday, as we sat on a wall outside Penn Station, having a quick slice of pizza in the few minutes before I had to get my train. "We may not have the car yet, but I have a plan."

I'd just been telling him how Miss Hauptman had found me a quartet. "They're a really good group," I'd said. "She says the coach is one of the best teachers at the conservatory. The only reason there's this opening is their cellist just broke her wrist. 'Which is unfortunate for her,

Sarah,' " I imitated Miss Hauptman's dry delivery, " 'but works out beautifully for us.' "

"When is it?" he'd said immediately.

"Next week. At two, I think. Oh, yeah," I added, trying to skim lightly over it, "and she also wants me to be at the next cello workshop. We're going to play all sorts of cool duets and trios and quartets."

Which is when he'd sneaked in his little bombshell. "Emily's been saying how she misses you," he started. "I told her you wanted some time with her, too. It's true, isn't it?" I nodded. "I also happen to know my dad will not be home Easter weekend. Stacy/Tracy, unbelievable as this may sound, thinks he's cool. So, my little Brussels sprout"—he picked up my hand and kissed it—"make sure you have no pressing musical events, because Emily's going to invite you for that weekend."

My pulse, which had barely returned to normal from all the kissing in the taxi, began to race again. "You're talking about two weeks from now," I said. "You're figuring out when. I'm still trying to deal with whether."

"It's just a suggestion." He stroked his thumb across my palm, which sent a wave of shivers down my back.

"David, this is way too weird for me, sitting here eating pepperoni pizza, talking about this stuff."

"Okay, I'll change the subject. Remember the Rodrigo piece I played for you?"

I nodded. "I love that piece."

"I'm arranging it for cello and guitar. So we can play together. You thought I was just kidding about that. It was going to be a surprise, but I'm not that great at keeping my mouth shut. Plus, I can use a little help with it, since I don't know that much about the cello." He took my other hand. "See what you think when you come over a week from Saturday."

"David!" I punched him. "I thought we'd changed the subject."

"We have."

"We have not."

"You told me you didn't want to slide into it, right? Or be pushed into it without knowing what you're doing? You wanted it to be a thought-out, rational decision. So here's a plan. You won't be pushed into anything. I promise."

"It also isn't fair to Emily. It's called using her."

"She'll understand. She's growing up, you know. She's got some guy calling her up, wanting to take her to the seventh-grade dance."

"Emily?" I couldn't believe it.

He nodded. "Puberty has struck."

"In the last month?"

"In the last week. Plus, she really does want to see you. I didn't make that up. She wants you to come over. That's how I thought of it. You should get a look at her, too, while her hair's still blue."

"She dyed it blue?"

"Azure. Cerulean. It's actually sort of an improvement."

"Why didn't she tell me?"

"Call her and ask her. Then we don't have to wait for her to call you. You can get her to have Florence call your parents to work it out." That earned him another punch. "By the way," he added, not quite looking at me, "did I tell you Michelle called?"

"No," I said. "You didn't."

"Yeah. The other night."

I was speechless.

"She said her family's coming to New York over Easter. I doubt that I'll see her, though. Since that's the weekend I'll be with you."

Chapter 18

Okay, so maybe I'm not the swiftest person in the world. Maybe it takes me a long time to figure out what's going on. Maybe if I'd known what I was feeling sooner, I wouldn't have done what I did. It still overwhelms me when I think about it.

"Excuse me, 'scuse me. Sorry." I pushed my way back through the crush of people vying for seats on the train. "Pardon me. I *said* excuse me. Sorry." Clutching the cello tight against my side, I bucked the crowd, ran up the escalator, and rushed back out into Penn Station.

It was only a few minutes since I'd left David, but there was no sign of him. I looked at the throngs of people milling around, blocking my view. My eyes darted from one to another—families with suitcases, shoppers, bag ladies—scanning the newspaper stands and fast-food places on the far walls. I figured he'd be going toward the subway, so I started running in that direction.

Try running with a cello in a hard case. It's not fun. "Wouldya watch it!" someone growled as he got bumped with it. "Yo. Watcha got there, girl?" some other guy called out. "That's a pretty big guitar."

I was almost ready to give up when, far off down the passageway, I recognized that unmistakable hands-in-the-pockets, tense-but-loose, almost-cool Friedman walk. "David!" I shouted, picking up my pace. "David!" I was getting closer but my yell disappeared amid the din. "David Friedman!"

He turned, a surprised but pleased look on his face. But as I got nearer, his smile vanished. "What's up?" he said. "Why aren't you on the train? What happened?"

"You just have to have what you want when you want it, don't you, David," I said, struggling to catch my breath. "You're saying it's up to me, but it's not up to me. You've completely boxed me in."

He couldn't have looked more shocked if I'd leaned over and bit him.

I was shocked myself. I never erupt. It's not something I do. But I went off like Mount Vesuvius, and once I'd started, I couldn't stop. "You're a baby, David. You're the biggest baby that ever walked the earth. A baby and a bully, just like your mother. No, worse, because with Florence, at least you know what you're getting. You know she's a bulldozer. She just rolls right over you. You, on the other hand, come on all sweet and ironic and funny and delightful and agreeable and sexy and sensitive and vulnerable. Look at you now, like you don't know what I'm talking about, and I know if I don't watch out I'm going to feel like I've wounded you for life and before I know it, I'll be saying, 'Oh, David, forgive me, I didn't mean to hurt your precious feelings. Do you need me to jump in bed with you to make it up to you?' "

David turned and started to walk away, but I grabbed his arm. "Where are you going?" I demanded.

He stopped and wheeled around, but he didn't meet my eyes. "I'm leaving." His voice sounded like someone was gripping him around the neck. "I don't see how I can be with you anymore."

"Why not?" I said. "Didn't anyone ever get mad at you before? No, probably not. Because you're also spoiled. You're so spoiled it's pitiful. Oh yeah, and by the way, I'm not your little Brussels sprout, David. I'm a cellist."

"Well, I hate to tell you, Sarah," he said, his voice so tight I hardly recognized it. "To be a cellist the way you think you're going to be, like all your wonderful new friends, you'd have to have started when you were three. So you can forget it. It's never going to happen. You think I'm pitiful, you're just another pathetic wanna-be."

He wrenched out of my grasp and, without looking back, he walked away.

I hate to cry. I hate feeling so helpless and humiliated and alone, especially when I'd started out feeling so enraged and powerful. And right.

I held it together the whole time I was in the station. But once I'd found a train—the train I was supposed to take was long gone—and sat down and pillowed my jacket behind my head, the tears came and wouldn't stop.

I couldn't face my family in that state, so when I got off, I picked up my cello and walked home. It's a long walk from the station, and a November-like drizzle had begun to fall, but that was fine with me. "Go ahead and ground me," I told my parents when I walked in the door. "You can ground me for the rest of my life and it won't bother me a bit."

They tried to find out what had happened, but I went up to my room, pulled off my wet clothes, and climbed under the covers.

After a minute, though, I got up and called David.

I see now that that was a mistake. I probably knew it then, but, once again, I felt swept into it, totally impelled, even though I had no clue what I was going to say or he'd say back.

The instant I heard his voice, though, heard him say in that stiff, injured way, before I could get a word in, "It's hard for me, Sarah. I need more than I'm getting. I know you don't think so, but you can be a pretty selfish person," I was furious again.

"If you want to break up with me, that's one thing," I told him, "but you had no business saying that about the cello. You have no right to be cruel."

"Yeah, well," he said, "those things you said to me weren't exactly kind."

"Well, you pushed too hard," I said.

"I wanted our relationship to progress." He sounded

really pompous. "Nothing can stay the same, Sarah. You move forward or you die. That's life. That's the way it is."

"Thank you, Dr. Friedman. Thank you for sharing that with me."

"You know, it's very hard to just have you in little dribs and drabs," he said.

"Why do I feel like I always have to apologize to you for having something I care about—"

His voice rose. "And why do I always have to be the one who understands, who has to fit into everybody else's life!"

"Well, maybe if you had a life . . . ," I said.

People say venting your anger makes you feel better. It did, for about thirty seconds. Once I was off the phone, though, I felt sick to my stomach. And bruised, as if the whole length of my insides had been scraped with a potato peeler. I wrote that in a letter to him that I immediately destroyed.

It didn't help at all that I knew he felt the same. "He's hardly come out of his room since yesterday," Emily informed me. She'd called Sunday night to find out what was going on. I told her. Not about the sex part, but the rest of it. "It's worse than with Michelle," she said. "Much worse. He's not even playing the guitar."

"Yeah, well," I said, "I'm not exactly having a great time."

And it didn't get better as the week went on. Needless to say, he didn't call. The cello sounded as if he'd put a curse on it—whuffly, dry, and scratchy, hideously out of tune. I'd take it out, fight with it a few minutes, then pack it up again. At school, couples were coming out of the woodwork. Everywhere I turned, I saw them—kissing, touching, happy, easy with each other—making me wonder if I was the stupidest person who ever lived. But what got to me the worst, the thing that made me cry again, was the idiotic song. I woke up one morning with it in my head and I couldn't shake it. It was sung to the tune of "Oh, Christmas Tree":

> Oh Tim the Toad, oh Tim the Toad
> Why did you jump into the road?
> You used to be so green and fat
> And now you are so red and flat.

There were other verses, too, about Jake the Snake and Somebody the Cow. It made me think of David and his pathetic funeral-march "Rudolph," how I'd never reminded him of that, told him how it had made me like him instantly. We'd have laughed about it. We could have laughed now about the stupid things you fix on when your heart is broken. If only I hadn't screwed things up.

"What are you talking about, screwed things up?" Emily kept telling me. "He needed to hear those things. C'mon, Sarah, it's about time somebody said that to him. He is a baby and a bully. I just wish I could've heard you."

"Right, and now I've lost him."

"Seems to me it's more like he's lost you," she said.

But Friday night, she told me that Michelle had called. "Florence told me," she said, whispering. "She listened in after she answered the phone. She said Michelle's coming to New York."

"I know," I said. "He told me."

"She wants to see David the week after next. She asked if he was, quote, 'with anyone.' "

"And what'd David say?" I felt as if I couldn't breathe.

"Florence didn't tell me his exact words. I mean, she still doesn't know about you guys, so that part of it didn't mean that much to her, but I gather he said no."

"Did he say anything else?" I wasn't sure I could deal with the answer.

I could tell Emily didn't want to tell me. "I think they're, like, meeting someplace," she said finally. "I think it's, like, at some hotel."

Chapter 19

"I don't think he'll really see her," Emily told me for at least the fifteenth time. It was the next day, Saturday. I'd come in early, supposedly so we could meet outside her building and talk some more before my lesson, but I was sick of talking. "You haven't even said a word about my hair," she said, after we'd walked all the way to Riverside Drive without my talking. We'd gone in that direction to avoid running in to David, but I'd only worn a sweatshirt, despite my mother's protests, and the wind blowing off the Hudson River had me shivering.

"What about it?" I said, trying to blink a dust speck from my eye. The wind, aside from being damp and freezing cold, was whipping up old cigarette butts and plastic bags and dirt of every size and shape and aiming it all straight for my face.

"Its blueness," Emily said. "It's blue, remember, Sarah? Did you even notice?"

"Oh, right." It was, in fact, extremely blue. "It's cool. Do you have a tissue?"

"No, sorry." She looked at me closely. "You know, maybe you should just call him and be done with it."

"And say what?"

"I don't know. If you're that upset, you could always try apologizing. We know that's all he's waiting for."

"Why do you keep saying I'm upset?" I said. "I'm angry. There's a difference. Plus, why do you want me to apologize, when (a) I'm right, and (b) I thought you were against this whole relationship. I mean, you told me from the beginning it was a bad idea. I was just too big an idiot to listen to you."

"*Woof!* Sarah! Stop talking like that."

I looked at my watch. "Great! Now, on top of everything, I'm going to be late." We headed back toward Broadway. "Not that it matters, for all the practicing I did. I can't even play the cello anymore." As we got close to the conservatory I noticed a guy carrying a violin case. "Oh, no!" I groaned. "I was supposed to get the music for that quartet this afternoon. Beethoven Opus 18. I was supposed to learn my part. I don't know why I'm even going to this stupid lesson."

It wasn't a great lesson. "Intonation, Sarah!" Miss Hauptman scolded, irritable from spending ten minutes hunting down the music for me. "That D-sharp has been out of tune every time you've played it." Then a minute later, "Up-bow, Sarah! I just showed you that! If you start down-bow, you'll get tangled up. I'm sure they're going to take this movement fast, and they're not going to want to stop for you every three measures. That's why we're writing in the bowings and going over hard parts, so you can keep up with the others."

The Others, who no doubt had been playing since they were three. I slumped back in my chair. "I can't do this," I said. "I shouldn't even play with them."

"It's a bit late for that," she said. "They can't very well have a quartet without a cellist. What's going on, Sarah?"

"David and I had a fight," I said. "We broke up last Saturday."

"I'm sorry to hear that," she said, marking some fingerings on the part.

I took a deep breath. "He said I could never be a cellist because I didn't start when I was three. He called me a pathetic wanna-be."

She put her pencil down and looked at me. "Then no wonder you got rid of him," she said. "With friends like that, as they say, who needs enemies?" She didn't say it meanly, just decisively. She'd written him off. Eradicated him. The finality of it made my insides ache.

"That's not all there was to it," I said. "It was a lot more complicated."

"It always is," she said. "Let's try it again at letter H. And I strongly suggest you find an empty practice room after we're done and go over some of these trouble spots between now and two o'clock."

I did it, since I had no place else to go, but it's not easy practicing a cello part in a quartet. You don't have that many melodies to work on. It's more like little snippets, or a bunch of isolated notes, so it's hard to know how the piece sounds or what you're doing or if you're getting better. It's especially hard when you're feeling pushed into it by someone who has no appreciation of what you're going through. And when you're lonelier and more wretched than you've felt in your entire life.

I'd probably have blown the whole thing off if she hadn't come into my practice room at two and walked me to the room where the quartet was meeting. I shouldn't have been surprised which room it was: the exact scene of my humiliation with the cello group. "I don't know if I'm ready for this," I said, as the temperature of my hands dropped at least fifty degrees.

"You'll see," she assured me. "You'll be fine. You'll like working with Mr. Nicholas."

Mr. Nicholas was a small, baldish guy in black jeans and a black T-shirt and a thin ponytail. He did start the first movement really fast. And the others were exactly what I'd feared: I could tell from the first note, the way they came in as if they were one instrument. Mr. Nicholas, meanwhile, sang, conducted, walked around us, smiling, gesturing, nodding, cajoling, scolding. "Short! Crisp!" he'd say, snapping out the words to show us what he meant. Then, "Shhh!" patting the air with both hands. "Sneak in. Like a whisper. Is that really how you want it to sound?" The others would all shake their heads, though I could see nothing they were doing wrong. "No, no, Edward!" he cried, after the first violinist had done something I thought was great. "That's boring. That's pedestrian. It's ordinary. Show him, Pamela," getting a smug smile from the second violinist.

They barely even looked at me.

Here they were, the musicians David had been warning me about, the ones who'd been playing since they were in diapers. Edward looked barely out of diapers now, or maybe he was simply short. Pamela was another Natalie—extremely good and made sure everyone knew it. Zack, the viola player, didn't seem as stuck up, but he, too, was more like the level of the people in the cello workshop than my level. They all were. All Mr. Nicholas had to do was sing something once and they'd do it. Perfectly.

I'd thought he might go easy on me, since I was just filling in, but that only lasted for the first five minutes. Then it was, "Eyes up, Sarah! Look alive! Keep your eyes on the other players. Sarah, watch Edward." There were so many things to pay attention to, by the end of the first page I was almost drooling. "Sarah, you're worrying too much about the notes," he said. "*Pianissimo* means soft, not mousy. You're the foundation of the group. We need to know you're there. Play out!"

The thing is, it's kind of hard to play out with the words *pathetic wanna-be* echoing in your head, not to mention memories of the cello workshop, where I'd played out, all right, and thought I was doing really well, and then *splat!* It would have helped, too, if Pamela hadn't kept leaning over to check my part, giving me these looks as if I'd forgotten to use deodorant.

I also could not get into this quartet, which sounded like four prissy old ladies at a tea party. "Tim the Toad" was more my thing.

So the second movement floored me. It started with this sort of heartbeat in the lower voices—muffled, far away—while high above, the first violin spun out a plaintive melody. Then, suddenly, I had a solo. I didn't know at first it was a solo because of how it sneaked in under the violin, but Mr. Nicholas called out, "Sarah, you're on! Now save your bow!" I struggled to keep the sound going for twelve beats. "Save, save, build, build, crescendo! Yes!" It had to be the longest note known to man. Then, for a few measures, I took up the theme. "Yes, Sarah!" he cried again. "Keep it going! Now keep that intensity but slowly fade away. It's like a sigh."

I faded away before I'd really gotten the idea of it. But he'd meant those yeses, I could tell, and as Zack's and my lines began to move in harmony, I felt Zack paying more attention to me, imitating what I was doing. I was really listening now, trying to really play, not just keep from sinking. I tried to echo the others' phrasing, match their sounds, respond to everything they did. And this movement was no tea party. It was more like a gigantic mood swing, so sad in the beginning that my throat tightened. Then total calm, then sad again, then calm, then sad, the sad parts each time becoming rougher, darker, and more anguished.

But there was something really irritating about the way they played it. We got to this one part where the violin had that soaring theme and I had this sort of low, dark undercurrent, and I was playing mine the way it felt to me, like an angry mutter, building up a head of steam, and there were the others still playing as if they were wearing monocles and powdered wigs.

At letter Y, I got to play the theme again. And suddenly I couldn't have cared less if they'd been playing Beethoven since nursery school. I didn't care if I wasn't at their level. These guys knew nothing. They didn't get it. They were wusses. This movement was sad, yes, but it wasn't wimpy sad, lie-down-and-die-type sad. This was pissed-off music: crabby, stormy, grab-you-by-the-throat music. It made me feel like roaring.

So I roared. From somewhere at the very bottom of me, somewhere so deep I'd only guessed that it was there, I made my cello roar—a lonely, infuriated, disappointed, grief-filled roar.

But then the piece was over and I felt that I'd just gotten started. "Mr. Nicholas?" I said. My voice, surprisingly, sounded normal. Strong, even.

"Nick," he said. "Most people call me Nick."

"You think we could go back so I can try my first solo part again? I can do it a lot better."

He came over behind me and put a hand on my shoulder. "Whaddaya say, guys?" he said. "Sarah wants to do it again. Should we play through it one more time from the beginning?"

I couldn't see his face, but the others were all looking at me. Not with, like, reverence or awe or anything, but definitely looking at me. Sizing me up. Not dismissing me. And I knew—though I didn't need them to tell me. I'd known since letter Y.

David was wrong.

Chapter 20

I *could* be a cellist. I'd get so good he'd not only eat his words, he'd gag on them.

The whole time I practiced that night, I thought about Nick's words as we were finishing. "You've got a nice sound, Sarah. A real chocolate sound." I'd have loved telling David. But, of course, he didn't call, and there was no way I was calling him.

"He shaved all his hair off," Emily told me on the phone that week. "It looks really terrible. I mean, some people look okay with no hair, but not, like, if their head comes to a point. You should see it. Seriously. All he needs is a yellow shirt and he'd look like a number-two Dixon Ticonderoga."

"Good," I said. "Serves him right." Though I'd always loved David's hair.

"I keep thinking he wouldn't have done that if he's

really going to see Michelle. Unless he, like, wears a hat."

"Emily, I keep telling you," I said. "It's not like I'm lying in bed memorizing the telephone book. I have enough in my life without your brother."

"Sorry," she said. "Now *I'm* being like Florence. So what are you going to do over spring vacation?"

"Practice," I said. "A lot of practicing." It could take years before my technique caught up with the guys in the quartet, but I could handle that. That was just work. I already had the sound and the fire. That was another of Nick's words: fire. Or maybe he didn't say that till the next week. Or maybe I heard it from Miss Hauptman.

"Mr. Nicholas said some good things about you," Miss Hauptman reported at my next lesson. "He thinks you can fit in really well."

"With them?" I said. "The superstars? He said that?"

"Oh, it will be a stretch," she said. "You'll have to work hard to keep up." I nodded, still not quite believing it. "But there's nothing like playing with people better than you to make you improve very fast. And the summer session will be marvelous for you."

"Summer session?" I hadn't thought past spring vacation. I'd stopped thinking about summer after all that talk with David about moonlight on deserted beaches.

"Why do you think I wanted you to do well last week?" she said, giving me the look that, a few months before, I'd have called her beady-eyed stare. "I wasn't only being mean and heartless. Mr. Nicholas directs a wonderful summer string program. I never thought you'd be ready for it this year. It's at a glorious old hotel upstate. Musicians come from all over, not just the conservatory, and we have quartets, trios, string groups of every sort—"

"You'll be there, too?" I interrupted.

"Oh, yes, it's great fun. And after last week, I'm sure he'd like you to go up there with them."

"Is the whole quartet going? What about their other cellist?" I worried suddenly that I'd be bumping her.

"I assume she'll be there, too. Remember, there's always room in the world for another good cellist."

I thought I might explode from happiness.

She smiled, then leaned over and began digging in her bag. When she straightened up, she was smiling even more. "Look what I found when I was cleaning," she said, holding out a videotape. "They filmed Casals at Prades, playing 'Song of the Birds.' I thought you might like to borrow it over the vacation."

"Thanks!" I said. I felt a brief, sharp flash of sadness, remembering the day I'd played the piece for David, remembering that night he'd first told me about it on the phone; but as she handed me the tape, pride took its place. Miss Hauptman wanted to give me something. My teacher had given me a gift.

The pride and happiness stayed with me all through the quartet, even though we didn't get to the second movement this time. And Nick did bring up the summer program, though he called it camp. He even gave me the application to show my parents. "You can let me know after the spring break," he said.

"You should really come," Zack, the viola player, said, as he walked with me to the subway. He was sort of goofy-looking, compared to David, but he had soft brown eyes and a nice mouth. "The music's great and there's this, like, fantastic lake, and canoes. You ever go out in a canoe at night?" I shook my head. "Last year a few of us sneaked the canoes out and went over to this little island and there were, like, all these shooting stars and one of the guys brought his guitar . . ."

I felt another sting of sadness at his mention of the guitar, but I immediately shoved it back. "That sounds good," I said.

My parents thought it sounded good, too. They filled out all the paperwork.

It was great to have my life back in my control.

I managed to keep things in control that entire week. I even studied for my midterms. My report card didn't turn out that well, which sort of pissed off my parents, but I told them I was going to be a cellist and cellists didn't need all As. I was practicing so much they seemed to go for it. Practicing was really useful for a lot of things.

It kept me going until Saturday, the first day of the vacation, when suddenly I had no interest in getting out of bed. I still had the covers up around my ears at noon, telling myself I really needed the sleep, when Emily called.

"Don't say it," I said practically before she'd said hello. "I don't even want to hear his name. I don't want to know where he is or what he's doing."

Even I knew I was lying. This was the day David was supposed to meet Michelle.

"I'm not calling about David," she said. "It's Florence. I hate her so much. I wish I could just stay in my room for the rest of my life and never see her big, fat, ugly face again."

"What'd she do now?" I said, but I didn't listen to the answer, because I suddenly had the best idea I'd had in weeks. "Come out here," I said. "Your school's on spring break, too, right? Come stay with me. You could come right now." I could practice just as well with Emily around.

It took the rest of the afternoon and four more phone calls to work the whole thing out, but Florence finally agreed that Emily would arrive on the train Sunday and we'd pick her up. I was just reading her the timetable, in fact, when I heard my father's voice. "Sarah, come down here!" he called.

"I'm on the phone," I yelled.

A minute later he was knocking on my door. "Call whoever it is back," he said, coming in. He had a strange look on his face. "Have you been talking to people in Penn Station?"

"No, why?" I said, baffled.

"Because there's some religious guy here to see you."

"What do you mean, religious guy?" I said. "I haven't talked to anybody."

"All I can tell you," my father said, "is that there's a guy outside who claims he knows you and he's as bald as an egg."

Chapter 21

"Hi," David said.

"What are you doing here?" I said. I'd come out onto the front stoop but was sticking close by the open door.

"I came to see you," he said, not quite looking at me.

"Your hair looks terrible," I said. He looked smaller without his hair—undressed, unprotected, his scalp pitifully pale and shiny in the bright, late afternoon sun. I could see why my dad thought he might be from some religious group.

But before he could say anything, my parents appeared behind me. "Sarah, wouldn't you and your friend like to come inside?" my mother suggested, giving him her hostess smile, "instead of standing on the doorstep?"

"We're okay," I said. But they stayed there waiting till I introduced them. I could see my mother struggling to accept that this bald person was the famous David. I guess I had them partly trained, though: introductions over, they went back inside and closed the door.

And then, there we stood. Across the street the neighbor's kid rode up and down the driveway on his tricycle, and two doors down Joey McDermott waxed his car. David seemed to be looking at my feet. My big toe was poking through. "I have a hole in my sock," I said.

"I probably do, too," he said.

"I thought this was the day Michelle was coming in," I said.

"Yeah," he said. "It was."

"So then why aren't you with her?"

"I was. I left and came here." He tore a leaf off the juniper beside the steps and started meticulously pulling it apart. "It was so weird."

"Can you not do that, please," I said, when he'd finished shredding the first leaf and torn off another. "Can you please not destroy the shrubbery."

"I met her in the lobby of the Sheraton," he said, still not looking at me. "She was with her parents, and they were, like, all dressed up, and we just sort of sat there. They wanted me to go to the Empire State Building with them and to some corny restaurant for dinner and then go see the Easter Show."

"Is that why you left?" I said. "Because you couldn't be alone with her?"

"No. That's what was so weird. It was like I'd never known her. I mean, she seemed all right. She still had great hair. But that's all she was, just some person with great hair. She was nothing to me. Not even someone I'd want for a friend."

"You don't exactly know a lot about being friends," I said.

He didn't say anything. "So you came all the way out here to tell me this?" I said.

"No." He swallowed so hard I could see his Adam's apple. "I came to say I'm sorry."

My heart suddenly felt as if it didn't fit inside my chest. "Yeah, well, tell it to the bush," I said, nodding toward it. "Maybe my rhododendron wants to hear it."

He was trying to smile, but it wasn't working that well. "I don't usually talk to bushes," he said. "What am I supposed to call it?"

"It doesn't matter."

He leaned his hands on the iron railing, facing away from me. He cleared his throat. "Listen, Bush," he said. "Ms. Bush. Mr. Bush. Ex-President Bush," turning to me to see if I was smiling yet. I wasn't, which meant he had to go on. "I'm sorry I said the things I said. I'm really sorry about how I acted. I'm sorry about everything. Would you please tell her I just want her back? Would you ask her what I have to do to get her back? . . . "

"Tell it you're a real horse's ass," I said, trying to stop the quaver in my voice.

"I am. I know. Listen, Sarah . . . " It was the first time he'd called me by my name. I pulled off a hunk of juniper and had begun shredding it before I realized what I was doing and let it drop. He didn't notice. "Can we forget the bush and go for a walk or something?"

"I'm not wearing any shoes," I said. But I went and got them and told my parents we'd be back in a while.

We started walking up the block. "Let me explain something to you, David," I said. I'd waited three weeks to tell him this and nothing, not even this thudding in my chest, was going to stop me. "Something you probably don't want to hear, but I'm going to tell you anyway. The whole time we were together and I kept getting better with the cello? I thought it was because of you. I thought it was love that let me do it. Loving you." I'd started trembling even before I'd said the word, yet I had to tell him. "But I kept thinking about what I said to Emily about the math music, when she'd solved those inequalities. I told her: 'It's not Bach. It's you. *You* did it.' Well, it wasn't love that did it with the cello, either." I stopped walking and faced him. "I did it. Me. Sarah. Myself."

"I see. You figured out you didn't need me and *wham!* You dumped me."

I knew that wasn't what I meant, but I couldn't let myself get sidetracked. "Maybe you couldn't deal with Juilliard, David. You hated it there, I know. But I'm not you. I love the conservatory. And maybe I *can* fit in. I'm going to try. Even if you don't want me to. Even if all you want is for me to be your little Brussels sprout . . ."

"I never said little," he said. "Besides, that was a joke." He reached for my hand. I ignored it. "You sound so different, Sarah. Like you don't love me at all. I feel like I don't know you anymore."

"Hey," I said. "In the famous words of David Friedman, you move forward or you die."

"I was just talking about sex when I said that."

"Yeah, well, it applies."

We started to walk again. "I know why I said that thing about the cello," he said, kicking at a pebble. "It's not 'cause it was true. It's just, when you rushed up to me in the station that way and said those things about me, I lost it. I freaked. I got scared." He gave the stone another kick, and another. "I never said anything to you, but it scared me every time I had to meet you there at the conservatory."

I looked at him. "You're kidding. Why?"

He looked away. "I don't know. I guess I was afraid you'd see all the guys there and you wouldn't want me anymore, afraid you'd leave me for some hotshot cellist."

"This has nothing to do with any hotshot cellists," I said, "except possibly me, contrary to what you may believe." It was getting harder to hang on to the anger.

"But I don't think I'm the only scared one around here, Sarah." He kicked the stone into the storm drain. "I've been thinking maybe you, like, started the whole fight because you were scared about making love with me."

I began to get that seashell booming in my ears. "That's not true! You just made me really angry." But even as I protested, a corner of my mind had started wondering. I hadn't given that much thought to David's side of things. It hadn't dawned on me that he could be scared. What if he was right about me, too? I wondered if maybe I should apologize.

We had walked all the way to the elementary school at the end of the street when I said, "So why'd you do it, shave your hair off?"

"I guess I just wanted to make something different, change something. I look like a geek, right?" He pushed open the gate and walked into the empty playground. I followed him as he looked around at the slide and swings and jungle gym.

"I used to love that merry-go-round," I said. I walked over and gave it a shove. It began to turn. "I can't believe how small it looks now. My mother used to have to drag me off it. I'd stay on till I almost puked."

David ran his hand along the edge, and when it creaked and wobbled to a stop, he sat down. I hesitated, then sat next to him. We didn't say anything. Then he reached over and took my hand. "Callouses are coming along," he said, rubbing his thumb across my fingertips. "You must be getting really good."

"You don't look like a geek," I said.

And then, I'm not sure how, we were kissing. He stood up and pulled me to my feet and we kissed some more. Then he slipped his hands inside my shirt and then we moved down to the grass and he pressed me into the cool ground. I can't tell you the relief I felt being back in his arms, how comfortable it was, how familiar, how right.

I felt like sobbing.

"That feels really good," he said into my neck as I rubbed my hand over his scalp. I nodded. "But I'm going to let it grow again. It won't take long. Now that I know you still love me. Now that I have you back."

He rolled over and put his arm around me and drew me close. We lay looking up at the sky through the glossy new leaves on the maple tree. "I knew all along it wasn't love that was making you play so well," he said. "It would've been great if it *was* because of me, but I knew it was you."

Suddenly I needed him to know everything that had happened in the last three weeks. So I told him—about Nick, the quartet, the summer camp, and all about my solo in the second movement and how the other players just didn't get it. He got it. He knew exactly what I was talking about. He even knew Opus 18, Number 1. "But you're a guitar player," I said.

"Yeah, but sometimes I hear those quartets or the Beethoven piano trios and I start wishing I played the cello or the violin." He gave me an ironic look. "You think it's too late for me to start?"

My answer was a kiss.

"Know what I'm going to do?" he said when we finally broke apart. "I'm going to finish the Rodrigo for us. You think I'll have hair by next Saturday? Because I can definitely finish it by then."

"Oh, David. I've got the cello workshop," I said.

"I've got the whole vacation to work on it. Then Saturday, after your lesson, you can help me with the cello line, since I'm not that familiar with the cello. Plus, you can come in during the week. That's what we should do, 'cause my dad'll be at work. You're not doing anything this week, right?"

I told him Emily was coming out to spend the week with me, but that, too, didn't register. "You should just come in Monday," he said. "I'll still be bald, but you don't care because you love me. Right?" He leaned over and gave me a big kiss on the nose, which, for some reason, embarrassed me. "You really do, don't you?"

I nodded, but I was getting a feeling I couldn't push away, a horrible feeling way down in my stomach. "I told you, Emily will be here," I said again.

"She can come another time. She won't care," he said, kissing me again, kissing my neck, kissing me down inside my collar. "Oh, Sarah, I wish you wouldn't go away to that camp this summer. I wish you'd stay here with me."

Suddenly I couldn't breathe. "David, stop it!" I said. "Don't do this to me again."

He sat up, looking past me, not saying anything. "You're right," he said. "I am doing it again. This is what you meant about me, isn't it?"

"Yeah." I nodded.

"I didn't mean to do it, but I did it anyway, just like you said, just like a bulldozer. No wonder you hate me. I'm just like Florence."

"Yeah. You should have shaved your brain." But then

I sighed. "Oh, David, I don't hate you. And you're not like Florence. You're the greatest guy I ever met. But you won't stop pushing me." I watched as he broke off a dandelion and tied the stem into one knot, then another. "I feel like you want to own me, take me over totally. Like you don't recognize what's important to me if it isn't you." A thick lump was forming in my throat. "You can't seem to understand it, David, but I can't just be yours. I don't want to just be yours." I felt like throwing up. "I guess I'm saying that getting back together is a bad idea."

We got to our feet and started home. He looked so sad with his poor, naked head, I had to fight the urge to put my arms around him.

"So, what now?" he said, when we were almost at my door. "That's it for us? I get on the train and never see you again?"

"I don't know," I said. "That sounds so final."

He laughed harshly. "It sounds awful, is what it sounds."

I couldn't answer. I wasn't angry anymore, just so tired it was hard to move my mouth.

He reached in his pocket, pulled out his train ticket, and studied it as if it held the secrets of the universe.

I suddenly knew what Beethoven felt like when he wrote that second movement. Except I didn't have the heart for roaring. Only for crying. I didn't start, though, till he began to walk away. Then, as the tears came, I started up the path to my house.

I was almost at the steps when he called out to me.

"You really think," he said, coming after me, "that it's my goal in life to be a bully and a baby and a bulldozer? You think I want to screw up the best thing I ever had? You think I want to be like this? Or that I want to be like Elliott, walking away from everyone he cares about?" I'd seen David cold. I'd seen him angry and sarcastic, but I'd never seen him so upset. He looked about to roar. "So are you going to answer me, or am I going to have to ask the rhododendron bush?"

I still couldn't say anything.

He shook his head. "Forget it! This is too much like Florence and Elliott. I'm not even sure which one of them I am. I gotta leave."

I suddenly pictured him walking through the door with me. I pictured Shelley checking him out as I introduced him to her. "In New York, it's cool," I'd say, if she dared say a word about his head. Next thing I knew, I was imagining us in my room, wishing he'd brought his guitar so we could play together—if not the Rodrigo, then Bach as a duet, or "Three Blind Mice," or anything. I wasn't sure that in fifteen minutes we wouldn't get back into the exact same thing. I didn't know that this was ever going to work. I had no clue how you did this. But I said it anyway.

"David, wait."